The WITCH
of the
WHIRLWIND

THE SKY ELDERS

The WITCH
of the
WHIRLWIND

R.J. YOUNG

4 Horsemen
Publications, Inc.

4 Horsemen
Publications, Inc.

4 Horsemen Publications, Inc.
1497 Main St. Suite 169
Dunedin, FL 34698
4horsemenpublications.com
info@4horsemenpublications.com

Cover by J. Kotick
Typeset by Niki Tantillo
Edited by Kris Cotter

Library of Congress Control Number: 2023934261

Print ISBN: 978-1-64450-912-8
Hardcover ISBN: 978-1-64450-914-2
Audio ISBN: 978-1-64450-915-9
E-Book ISBN: 978-1-64450-913-5

DEDICATION

To my dear friend Jack. You helped me through one of the darkest periods of my life. I will be forever grateful. Thank you.

TABLE OF CONTENTS

HISTORICAL MAP
REFERENCES

Blue Patowa'Kacha: The Ocean
Bitter Root Valley: The Verde Valley, Arizona
Crystal Cave of the Spider Women: The
Cave of the Winds, Colorado
Earth Lodge: The Keweenaw
Peninsula, Michigan
Endless River Agazzi: The Mississippi River
Gitche Gumee: Lake Superior
Kolhu: Chaco Canyon, New Mexico
Land of Everlasting Summer: The Four
Corners region of CO, UT, AZ, NM
Lake Cle-Elum: Dream Lake, Arizona
Manitou's Rise: Manitou Incline, Manitou
Springs, CO

Norumbega: The Great Lakes Region
Pisas Vaya River: The Colorado River
Shining Rock Mountains: The
Rocky Mountains
Shipapa-Lina: Mesa Verde, Colorado
Ulah-Nane: North America
Vineland: The Gulf of St. Lawrence,
Eastern Canada

CHAPTER ONE

AD 1251—The Red Debi-Kway-Inan of the
Great Turtle's Trek

The wind can kill when the gods are angry. Tawa had been haunted by ominous dreams of violence before he was woken by the foreboding howl of the savage windstorm. Leaves blew into the entryway of the stone chamber, brushing against Tawa's face like a slap of challenge.

Tawa noticed his wife Pinga was also awake, lying pensively at his side. As he slipped out of their bed made of hay and feathers covered by animal skins, he smiled reassuringly at her.

"I can hear your fears whispering dire warnings to me, my love," he said. "No need for apprehension. You won't be sleeping alone tonight. Worry not. We have enough fear in our lives. Surely, we don't need to look for more of it. Fear makes our enemies loom larger."

"This One senses an unnatural wind," Pinga said. "Do not be recklessly brave, my beloved. Come back to me unharmed."

Tawa kneeled and kissed his lovely wife. "Haven't I always done so? You motivate me to miracles. Be at peace. I will return soon."

Tawa winked at her, then grabbed his sacred spear Dragonfly and hurried out into the wind. Pinga sat pensively for a few moments and then rose, putting on her garments. *Where is our son? He should be at his father's side.*

Tawa stepped out of his rock-hollow chamber on the cliffside and looked over his village of Shipapa-Lina. The Itiwana tribe had fortified their defenses using the clever new design Tawa had conceived of.

The Itiwana had meticulously constructed a form of cliff housing, constructed in shallow caves on the canyon walls on the west cliffs, shielded by a rock overhang above. This community housed six hundred structures made from stone and adobe. Some residential units were merely a single room, while others had as many as four or five apartments. The extraordinary dwellings were adequately protected from the elements, as well as from attackers. A series of ladders allowed the Itiwana to climb the cliffside. The ladders could be pulled up to prevent enemies from reaching the inhabitants.

Still, much of Shipapa-Lina was vulnerable to tornados. The crops, as well as the small outer farms, buffalo pens, the deep well, and the Sun Temple, had all been damaged on previous occasions by these preternatural windstorms. Even the sound of this wind seemed to be a wailing threat.

Tawa was now an experienced ruler who had seen thirty-eight summers go by. He was more well-muscled in his mature years than he had been back when he had become chieftain at the age of sixteen summers. His long hair blew in the gusts as he spotted what appeared to be a small cyclone in the distance. It was too small to be a natural tornado, but the wind was becoming oppressive. *Pinga is correct. This is not a natural wind. Is the witch back?*

The Itiwana felt the wind begin to strengthen rapidly. Tawa was unsure at first as he went to collect his massive bison, Mountain Fury. His concern increased as the wind grew ever more oppressive. It started to howl as if a storm were coming. The strangest part was that the sky and clouds had not changed at all. *I have seen foul weather before, but this is ... disconcerting.*

Looking below, he saw Aholi and Evaki riding urgently toward the cliff housing. Sitting atop Aholi's buffalo, Stone Horn, both were clearly upset. At the age of 50 seasons, Aholi had been the war chief of the Two Horn Riders since the death of brave Pogum 20 summers ago. Sitting behind him was his devoted but depressing wife,

Evaki. Aholi was the cousin of Tawa's missing father, Yana-Luha.

"We spotted the whirlwind approaching from the east," Aholi shouted up at Tawa, trying to be heard over the screaming winds. "We've warned the outer farms. The danger is approaching swiftly."

"It'll probably destroy everything this time," Evaki said with monotonous fatalism.

Pinga stepped out of the cave hollow and touched Tawa on the shoulder. "This One fears it is she. We must find our son."

"No time," Tawa said, restraining his anger about their son's absence at this critical time. "Pinga, you and Evaki make certain that everyone stays inside. Keep our people safe. And Evaki, let Pinga do the talking."

Evaki slid off Stone Horn. "As you wish, Kik-Mongwi."

Aholi smiled at her. "I will see you soon, my plum."

"Don't get killed, you big oaf," Evaki said.

Aholi chuckled at her expected surliness and signaled for his chieftain to come down from the cliff housing. "I will take you to your mount, Kik-Mongwi."

Tawa slid down the ladder and hopped onto the back of Stone Horn. "Go!"

Pinga and Evaki watched Tawa and Aholi ride off to battle. Pinga peered around the village, searching for some sign of her son. *Where are you, Pahana?*

The powerful gusts tore through the outer fences as the menacing roar of the winds became louder. The two warriors reached the buffalo pens and Tawa leaped onto his massive bison, Mountain Fury. Tawa had ridden the mighty bison since both were young. Twenty seasons later, Mountain Fury was not quite as fast as it used to be, but still the biggest, strongest bison in Ulah-Nane.

As he left the pen, Tawa spotted a large elk standing calmly nearby. The animal was seemingly unafraid of the approaching twister. The elk looked intently at Tawa with a meaningful stare.

"Manabazo, is that you?" Tawa asked, shouting over the yawp of the wind.

"It is I, as the kik-mongwi already knows," Manabazo said in his elk form. "I come when the wind of death blows."

"Is it her?" Tawa asked.

"I say yes to the leader of the Itiwana. I believe it is the witch, Dagwona."

Dagwona, the Witch of the Whirlwind, had been a plague on the Itiwana tribe for many years. This feud began centuries ago during a conflict between the witch and the legendary Morning Star. As a result, Dagwona angrily united with the Winter Elders, who promised her a small glen of eternal warmth that she could rule in the aftermath of the war between the Elders when they covered the globe in ice.

When the Winter Elders lost the previous war, Dagwona went into hiding for more than

200 summers. Fifty summers ago, she took on an apprentice who became the Salt Witch. Her apprentice subsequently became a worshipper of Malsumis and tried to assist in his resurrection by destroying the Tree of Life. She created the skin-walkers to help achieve this objective. The Salt Witch was killed by the Itiwana, and a vengeful Dagwona had therefore renewed her hostilities against the people of Shipapa-Lina.

Tawa nudged his bison forward, gesturing for Aholi to follow him. Now that the tribe had retreated to the cliff houses or the pit houses for safety, it was time to confront the enemy. He simmered with anger at his son Pahana for not being there when he was needed. The Itiwana had expected this attack for some time, and Pahana was supposed to be the one to deal with it. He had a special ability that the tribe needed, but Pahana was nowhere to be found. *Undependable child.*

Tawa and Aholi had to grab more tightly to their mounts; otherwise, the wind would have tossed them around like dry leaves. Even the massive bison were feeling threatened by the force of the wind, but the animals managed to push forward toward the small tornado.

Surprisingly, the wind stopped as suddenly as it had started. The mini cyclone vanished, only to be replaced by a woman. Tawa let go of the reins and studied the newly appeared female. She was tall, with a toned body and wild, wind-blown hair. She wore something that looked almost like brown armor, except that it was made of bark-wood: a soft, thick, slightly textured fabric made from the inner bark of certain trees. Tawa could deduce who this was, although he had never seen her in her corporeal form before now.

The strange woman glared imperiously at Tawa. "Ah, an adversary arrives as anticipated. Feeble foes foolishly flock forward."

"And here we are," Tawa said. "I suppose there are very few surprises left in life. I assume you are Dagwona."

"No names needed now," she replied. "Windswept warfare won't wait."

"I don't suppose you're willing to discuss this, are you?" Tawa asked.

"Idiotic idea!" she snapped.

"I thought as much," Tawa said warily. He tightened his grip on his spear, Dragonfly, wondering what the powerful witch would do next. As she took a step closer, he raised his weapon threateningly.

"You're powerful," Tawa said. "You're impressive. But so is my spear. Don't be rash. You'll look unattractive once impaled."

She narrowed her eyes menacingly. "Don't dare defy Dagwona!"

"Dagwona?" Tawa repeated. "So, it is you. The Witch of the Whirlwind finally reveals herself. What has earned us such an honor, Witch?"

"'Tis time to terminate the tribe," she replied. "Whirlwind Witch won't wait. Dagwona destroys directly!"

"Perhaps you will," he said. "But your loathsome disciple did not fare very well against us. We killed the Salt Witch. If you had trained her better, she might still be here. But she's not."

"Requiring ruthless revenge!" the whirlwind witch yelled angrily. "Shipapa-Lina shall surely suffer!"

Tawa thought for a moment, then lowered his spear. "No, I don't think so. Look at you. So mighty, so quick! Yet you stand there, sneering and talking. You are trying to intimidate me. If you were planning to kill me, you wouldn't have stopped your wind attack. You struck, and then you stopped. You are either a poor killer, or you never intended to hurt me. Not now, anyway."

"Why would Whirlwind Witch wait?" she hissed.

"Because you fear Awona'Wilona," Tawa said. "You and your fellow dullards who follow Malsumis have yet to free him. Until you do, you won't risk directly defying great Awona'Wilona by attacking Shipapa-Lina personally. Not while Manabazo is there. You don't want to fight him, or you will defy the divine ruling. That's why you and your den of detestable slugs have been using minions. You've never attacked the Itiwana directly. And you won't now!"

Dagwona's eyes seared into Tawa as if she were physically assaulting him. He prepared himself for an attack, just in case he was wrong in his assumptions. Fortunately for him, he was not.

"Dagwona doesn't directly destroy domains," she said. "Itiwana's inland is insignificant."

"If we're so insignificant, why do you keep coming back here, Witch?" Tawa asked.

"To torment tribes," she said. "Helpless humans huddle here."

"Helpless, you say?" Tawa questioned. "Enough voracious ants can devour a giant alive!"

"Stop speaking!" she yelled. "Mortal man makes mistake. Chieftain comes carelessly close. Very vulnerable."

"Perhaps I am vulnerable here," he said. "But I carry Dragonfly, and I defy you."

"As do I," Aholi shouted.

"We are united against you," Tawa said. "Will you withdraw, or do we battle?"

"Battle begins," the witch snarled. "Watch with wonder while Whirlwind Witch wins!"

Dagwona spread her arms as if to cast some enchantment that would destroy the leader of the Itiwana.

CHAPTER TWO

T he lethal winds howled, drowning out the vengeful cackles of the Witch of the Whirlwind. Her moment of vengeance was close.

However, before she could act, Pinga arrived. The albino beauty stepped from behind a protective wall and revealed herself to the kachina witch. Dagwona paused, apparently recognizing a Sky Elder.

"An ancient albino arrives," Dagwona stated, seemingly hesitant to attack an Elder, even a depowered one. "What would white woman want?"

Pinga stood calmly, with a regal bearing that hid her nervousness. "This One will not allow you to continue your carnage. It must stop now, and This One will stop you."

Dagwona paused, but only for a moment. She raised her hands as the winds began to wail even louder. "Fallen fool. Pitiful, powerless Pinga. Whirlwind Witch won't withdraw."

Tawa felt a wave of fear overcome him, seeing his bride confront the powerful witch. "Pinga, go back! Let me deal with this."

"This One will not flee," Pinga said. "She stands with her husband in defense of Shipapa-Lina. We two cannot fail together."

Tawa knew that Pinga had been stripped of most of her godlike powers. What little she did have were a chore for her to use. He worried when she was compelled to utilize her waning abilities. "Pinga, please. This is my duty as the kik-mongwi."

"And This One is the wife of a kik-mongwi," she said. "It is our duty."

Dagwona had lost her patience. "Touching tableau. Dagwona destroys devoted duo. Lovers lose lives."

A cyclone began to form around Dagwona, enveloping her in a gray swirl of dirt and dust. The mighty winds screamed angrily. Even Mountain Fury and Stone Horn felt the gusts assaulting their massive frames.

"No more," Pinga announced loudly.

Tawa saw the ground underneath Pinga begin to freeze. A sheet of ice spread from beneath her feet, covering the grass and soil of the Land of Everlasting Summer. The expanding ice encased the ground underneath the hooves of Mountain Fury and Stone Horn. The area of rime continued to grow. Pinga's lovely face grimaced with the strain of her labors.

The hoarfrost coated the ground underneath the witch and her whirlwind. Dagwona's eyes widened in alarm. She wasn't a winter spirit and had only begun her alliance with the followers of Malsumis for the sake of vengeance against the tribe of Pogum and Tawa. Cold was not her natural terrain.

Pinga's subzero attack injected an immense amount of cold air into the uptake area of Dagwona's storm center. The bitter cold depleted the chaotic intensity of the warm, humid air that spun through the whirlwind. The frosty updraft dissipated the specific air conditions necessary for Dagwona to spawn a tornado.

As the whirlwind vanished, Dagwona registered her shock. She evidently had not anticipated this possibility. "Inconceivable incident," she cried. "Beyond belief!"

While Dagwona stood confused, Tawa took the opportunity to target her with his sacred spear, Dragonfly. He aimed at his enemy and threw the spear with all the strength of his arm. The spear flew unerringly at the target, as it always did.

This time, unlike every previous occasion, the spear did not hit the target. Dagwona spotted Tawa lifting his arm to throw the weapon, and she instinctively reacted. A gale-force wind grabbed the spear and caused it to veer off course. Dragonfly missed the witch by mere inches.

Tawa could see the fear on Dagwona's face. The combination of Pinga's cold attack and the close call of Dragonfly was too much for her. She raised her arm again, and another intense funnel of wind manifested. The winds lifted Dagwona off the ground. She seemed to levitate toward the clouds, floating above the trees. Then a wind stream pushed her to the north faster than a bird could fly. Within a minute, Dagwona was gone from sight.

Pinga stood unsteadily on her feet, her strained breath visible as foggy water vapor coming from her panting mouth. Tawa could see she was disoriented. He urged Mountain Fury into motion. The big bison's weight cracked the ice underneath its hooves.

"Aholi, go fetch the Dragonfly for me," Tawa ordered as he rushed to Pinga's side. He was focused completely on his wife, who teetered unsteadily.

"You were spectacular, my love," Tawa said. "Are you well?"

Pinga looked at him with half-open eyes. "This One is ... weak."

As Tawa was climbing down from Mountain Fury, he saw Pinga listing to one side. Her eyes drooped closed, and she collapsed into a faint. Tawa's quick reflexes kept her from hitting the ground.

"Pinga, my dearest!" he cried.

He scooped up his unconscious wife and gently placed her onto Mountain Fury. Leaping up onto the mount, he compelled the bulky bison to begin running.

"Faster, large one," he yelled. "Ride like the wind."

The sound of hooves over ice gave way to a trail of dust over the grass field as Mountain Fury ran his fastest. As they approached the bison pens, Tawa saw the elk again.

"Manabazo, I need you!"

The residents of Shipapa-Lina were still sheltered in their dwellings, awaiting word from their leader. As part of their defense, the series of retractable ladders had been pulled up to keep attackers from climbing to the cliff chambers. Most of the cliff dwellings were residential, but some were for storage.

The impressive cliff palace, which was dubbed the Great Lodge of Shipapa-Lina, had been completed. The Shakowin regularly met there to discuss important matters and mediate disputes. It had become a symbol of the Itiwana's defiance of the Enemy Way.

Attacks by the Tunerak Destroyers or the skinwalkers had tapered off to only a few times per year, and even those attacks seemed to be half-hearted efforts by groups who no longer believed that they could win. Even when monsters such as Lucifee the Wildcat attacked, the cliff housing provided relative safety.

Despite the efforts of the followers of Malsumis, no one except Tawa had been able to find Yaxche, the Tree of Life. Anyone who went searching— even the mighty Gichi-Awas—was driven out of the Land of Everlasting Summer by the Two Horn Riders. Tawa had kept his word to protect the all-important tree.

Although the followers of the Enemy Way had made numerous attempts to free their lord Malsumis from his volcano prison, they had failed so far. The endless summer had weakened Malsumis too much, and Awona'Wilona's power was at its peak. The followers of the Enemy Way knew they had to find a way to destroy Yaxche but had repeatedly failed to find it. Only the Itiwana knew where it was, and they weren't sharing that information.

The symbiotic bond between the bison and the Itiwana had been sealed. The Itiwana tribe was thriving, thanks to the great bison and years of good corn harvests. Many Itiwana believed Awona'Wilona was looking out for them as a reward for their devotion and for protecting Yaxche.

The Shakowin oversaw Shipapa-Lina whenever Tawa was away. Since the passing of Old Pekwin, the current members of Tawa's Shakowin were T'Soona, Pinga, Manabazo, and Tawa's mother, Atira. His two children were being molded to fit future leadership positions.

Atira stood on the ledge outside her cliff chamber, looking nervously for any sign of her son Tawa. Despite her faith in his abilities, a mother could not help worrying. At the age of 56 summers, she had spent twenty-two of those seasons watching her son efficiently lead the Itiwana against a myriad of bizarre and deadly foes. He had overcome them all so far, but few were more powerful than the Witch of the Whirlwind.

Dagwona had attacked the Itiwana at approximately the same time every year, beginning several summers after Pogum slew her disciple, the Salt Witch. The Witch of the Whirlwind kept returning to create fear and damage as punishment for the Itiwana's sins. Her early attacks were devastating. It had taken some time before they concocted a defense.

Kia, daughter of Tawa and Pinga, had shown an affinity for eldritch powers, but was too young to master them. It was only recently, after Pahana developed his new, divine ability, that Tawa had come up with an idea for a defense. Pahana was meant to be here to defend the tribe.

That irresponsible young fool, Atira thought.

Atira's long tresses had begun to turn gray after decades of fretting over Tawa's safety. She let out a relieved sigh when she saw Mountain Fury and Stone Horn cantering toward the cliff housing. Tawa sat atop his mount, but he was carrying something. *What is it? That's a person. Who could it... It's Pinga!*

Tawa rode closer and called out to the tribe, "Everyone may come out now. The danger has passed. It's safe."

Tribe members began to appear from hiding. Atira lowered a ladder and climbed down to meet her son. "What's wrong with Pinga?"

"She did what Pahana was supposed to do," he said.

"That feckless boy," Atira replied. "What can we do for Pinga?"

"Manabazo says we can do nothing but let her rest," Tawa answered. "Find T'Soona. Perhaps he can do something to comfort her. Aholi, help me carry Pinga up to our dwelling."

CHAPTER THREE

Pahana rode his bison mount across the great plains of Ulah-Nane. The son of Tawa was now a man of 20 summers. Pahana had the same dark eyes and hair as his father, but possessed snow-white skin like his mother. Partly a Sky Elder and partly a mastop-kachina, Pahana was a very unusual being in this world.

He was being trained to become a leader and a warrior. Both his father, Tawa, and wise Manabazo were trying their best to prepare him for the day he would eventually become a chieftain, but his independent streak and burning desire to explore Ulah-Nane made him rebellious. Pahana was a fast learner and had become a cunning, formidable warrior. He had killed several

CHAPTER THREE

Tunerack Destroyers by the time he had reached the age of 18 summers. However, he still had a lot to learn.

Pahana had recently been declared the new chief of the hunt after the previous holder of that title was killed in an ambush by Lucifee the Wildcat while out hunting. Pahana had a natural authority but a certain enigmatic aloofness.

He urged his huge mount onward. The big bison was called World Giant. Pahana was followed by a pet wolf called Chybiabis, the spawn of Pinga's two lupine companion's Wind and Moon.

Pahana was not alone on the hunt. He was accompanied by two younger cousins. The pair were fraternal twins named O'Yewa and Masewa, the children of Aholi and woeful Evaki. They had reached the age of 18 summers. O'Yewa had inherited his father's cheerful, friendly demeanor and was known as Bright O'Yewa. Masewa had his mother's gloominess and was therefore called Dark Masewa. O'Yewa rode a bison mount called Lightning Charger, and Masewa rode atop Thunder Rumbler. The two were inseparably close, and they looked up to their elder cousin Pahana. All three of the young men worshiped Tawa.

The fourth man on the hunt was Calian. Pahana and his cousins were very closely bonded to Calian, son of Bluebird and the slain Pogum. At age 20 summers, Calian was practically the reborn image of his father, minus the minor scars. He even had the same streak in his hair. Like his father, Calian was a young man of many talents.

19

As Tawa had promised Bluebird long ago, the Itiwana people had all pitched in to help raise and mentor Calian.

The boy honored his father by listening to all of them. He learned everything there was to learn in Shipapa-Lina. Everyone described him as being wise beyond his age. He was frequently seen in the company of Pahana and the sons of Aholi. Calian was technically an uncle to Pahana, although no one referred to him that way because they were the same age. Calian's other constant companion was big Faw-Faw, the hirsute woodman who had dedicated his life to being Calian's protector.

Calian rode a mount named Walking Storm, just as his father's bison had been named. Calian also had a pet hawk given to him by Manabazo, which he called Spirit. Calian was more serious-minded than the sons of Aholi and more focused on the danger from the Enemy Way than Pahana seemed to be.

On this particular morning, Pahana, O'Yewa, Masewa, and Calian had gotten together for a hunting expedition. They were searching for the saber-toothed wildcat, Lucifee. The ferocious Lucifee was one of the poshayanki, like A'Chiyala the Sky Monster had been. Lucifee was a fierce beast who served Malsumis and the Enemy Way. The beast shied away from attacking the entire Itiwana tribe alone. Instead, it chose to destroy the Itiwana's food supply. Lucifee had been driving the large game away from the Land of

Everlasting Summer, as well as killing their hens and roosters.

On occasion, Lucifee would even attack the Itiwana's bison. For the most part, these specially bred, extra-large bison were able to defend themselves from such predators. But occasionally, the advantage of surprise, combined with the ferocity and massive fangs of Lucifee, allowed it to kill one of the big beasts. The Itiwana had not spent much effort to stop Lucifee until it killed the previous master of the hunt. Now that Pahana had taken up that mantle, he decided to make Lucifee a priority. Thus far, his efforts to find the beast had failed. Frustrated, the son of Tawa, along with his three stalwart companions, set out to deal with the creature personally.

The four young men mounted their steeds, World Giant, Walking Storm, Lightning Charger, and Thunder Rumbler, and set out with the fearlessness of youth to slay a poshayanki. Three among them were quite happy and confident. Calian was the exception. He knew they should be hunting food while leaving Lucifee to be dealt with by Aholi, the war chief, and his Two-Horned riders. Pahana, however, would not listen.

Pahana shouted to his kin, "What is better in life than earning glory in the company of good companions? Lucifee had best pray to his malevolent master Malsumis for assistance because the vile beast will lament his birth when we catch up to him... as we surely will. Ah, the joy of the hunt."

Calian sighed at Pahana's reckless enthusiasm. "If zeal were a weapon, Malsumis, and the entire Enemy Way, would be surrendering at your feet."

"Give me time," Pahana boasted mirthfully. "I'm still young."

Faw-Faw lumbered toward the foursome, intending to accompany them. Calian held up his hand. "You stay, my friend. I'll be fine. I'm in the best of company."

Faw-Faw cocked his head, taking a moment to comprehend the information. Calian made him understand, and the hirsute being headed back to the cornfield to help with the plowing.

"Shall we go?" Masewa asked. "Time is ebbing."

"Shall we race?" O'Yewa added. "From here to Stone Coat?"

"Wonderful thought," Pahana said. "Enjoy looking at the rump of World Giant as I leave you all in awe of my speed. I shall wait for you all at Stone Coat. Begin."

Pahana nudged World Giant into action, and the substantial bison sprinted forward. His wolf, Chybiabis, ran alongside. Laughing with youthful vigor, O'Yewa raced after him. Masewa followed along, determined not to be the last to Stone Coat. They kicked up a small cloud of dust and dirt. Calian had no option but to join in, although he felt they should be more focused and serious while hunting deadly Lucifee.

Tawa sat beside his unconscious wife in the Great Lodge cliff palace. Manabazo and T'Soona assured him that she would recover from her exertions, although they both stated she should not do what she did again. Tawa promised to stop her from doing so. He fumed with disappointed anger at Pahana.

Tawa had watched his son, cousin, and nephews race off for some youthful adventure. He had even smiled, assuming their hunt would merely be a brief jaunt where they would bond as warriors and quickly return. He had not expected them to be gone overnight.

Tawa liked to encourage these little adventures by the boys. He even envied their zest for life. Tawa hadn't felt such joyful passion since the day his father had to sacrifice himself, and Tawa was left with the weight of Shipapa-Lina on his shoulders. He mused on that long ago day and wished he could feel that unburdened happiness again. He hadn't been able to relax since the first moment he saw Achiyala so long ago.

In recent years, the brewing war was a limited affair, marked only by occasional skirmishes. However, the Sky Elders were immortal. Immortals viewed time in a quite different and unique way from mortals and were a patient bunch. A small delay to them was many seasons to a mortal. All the summers and winters that had passed for the Itiwana were merely the blink of an eye to the Elders from the skies. And the peace could end at any time. There was no predicting when things would become chaotic again.

It was best, therefore, to allow the young ones to enjoy their adventures now because the fun would most likely not last. However, enjoying youth and evading responsibility were two different things. Tawa was furious that Pahana's frivolous wanderings had endangered Pinga.

I have an apple to peel with that boy, Tawa thought angrily. *I'll see he learns some sense.*

Just outside of Shipapa-Lina, Pahana and his three kinfolks were racing toward Stone Coat. Calian had passed Pahana and taken the lead in the race. While Pahana's bison was a large and powerful beast, it was not as fast as it was strong. Calian's mount was a foot smaller and considerably lighter and, therefore, quicker and more mobile. Calian was the most skilled rider of the bunch, having dedicated himself to doing all the things that his father did so well.

Calian was the first to reach the immobile rock form of the being formerly known as Stone Coat. Calian always saw the presence of the defeated, unmoving Stone Coat as a symbol of family pride because it was his late father who caused the creature's defeat. Calian hoped he could serve his own people as ably as Pogum once did.

When he was overtaken by Calian, Pahana was embarrassed but also impressed by his uncle.

"Hah. That little beast of yours doesn't seem to touch the ground when he runs. I think you're secretly a mystic, like my sister."

"Better than that," Calian said. "I am the cousin of Tawa, uncle of Pahana, and son of Pogum. What more could anyone ask?"

"Well said," Pahana answered. "Perhaps speed is what we need to catch Lucifee."

Calian was perplexed. "I thought we were returning home? Isn't that why we raced toward the village?"

"Not without the head of that cursed wildcat!" Pahana insisted. "Should I return to my father with nothing but news of our failure?"

O'Yewa and Masewa came trampling along to join their elder cousin and uncle. They arrived almost simultaneously, although Masewa was a nose ahead. O'Yewa erupted in exuberant guffaws, despite coming in last. It didn't seem to bother him that they'd been beaten so badly.

"Tortoises," Pahana shouted to them, half-jok-ingly. "I cannot believe you are my kin. My young sister could outrun you snails. Come along and make your best attempts not to embarrass me further."

"I never do anything fast," O'Yewa replied. "And while we may be slow, we excel at guarding the rear."

"I hope my safety never depends upon you two racing to my assistance," Pahana taunted. "I hope your mounts are not too tired because we still have a goal to complete. Lucifee still walks the fields of Ulah-Nane. That makes me angry. I intend to make myself happy."

"More adventures?" O'Yewa asked, excited. "Excellent."

"I'm glad you approve," Pahana said sarcastically. "And please try to find some semblance of speed. I know I will likely see fish walk on land before you two impress anyone with your swiftness, but do your best to arrive the same day as Calian and I."

"Don't you ever get tired?" Masewa asked.

"Only when I stop," Pahana replied. "And as for you, Calian... Let me lead the way. You've battered my pride enough for one morning."

"I follow where you lead, as always," Calian said.

"Except when we're racing," Masewa commented.

"Jest later; ride now," Pahana ordered. "Come."

Pahana rode speedily toward Shipapa-Lina, with his three devoted companions close behind. Chybiabis ran energetically along with them. Their carefree, jovial mood would not last.

CHAPTER FOUR

Up north in Norumbega, the villages of Teketsertok and Vineland had called a truce. The Thrown-Aways and the Vykans had been at war for fifteen summers before the violence finally ended. The leaders of the two groups realized that the feud had to end. Angakku had gotten old and tired. He saw that his young Thrown-Aways were growing up and having families of their own. Children were being born in Teketsertok. Angakku didn't want a new generation growing up with endless combat, especially since Angakku was aware that his days were coming to an end. He didn't want to leave the responsibility of fighting the Vykans to someone else.

As for the Vykans, their leader Hunwulf was also starting to feel the turning of the years. And he was not the only one. His original group of Vykans were all past their prime. The long years of war had piled up many casualties, and his once formidable fighting force was no longer the fierce threat it used to be. The Vykan ranks had been boosted a bit by the addition of the Hee-Heez, women who were once part of a wandering clan of hunters, until most of their male kinfolk were killed by skinwalkers. Fleeing, they came across the Vykans, and the primal urges of the lonely, lusty Vykans led to them being accepted into the Norseman's home in Vineland. The women had a civilizing influence on the Vykans, and so Hunwulf decided to end hostilities.

Not long after Angakku and Hunwulf made a blood oath to keep the peace between the two sides, Angakku succumbed to an illness that had long afflicted him. His determination to protect his people had kept him strong, but once his purpose had finally been served, the great Angakku died, leaving Elder Brother to lead the Thrown-Aways.

Elder Brother had wed Nulia, who had become a mature woman and given birth to a child. The heir to the community's leader was named Angakku, like his grandfather, but was mostly called the Rabbit Hunter. As a mother and the wife of the tribal leader, Nulia had changed into a thoughtful, patient woman. She still retained her friendship with the Painted White Girl—who had become known as the Painted Woman—and had also become close to her friend's child Hayoka.

Hayoka, the son of Hobomok and the Painted Woman, had now seen twenty summers pass. He had been born the same day and hour as Pahana. Hayoka physically favored his mother, being thin and sinewy. He had also taken up his mother's habit of wearing face paint. When he was younger, and the Thrown-Aways were fighting the Vykans, his mother had encouraged him to wear war paint as the people of her extinct tribe, the Northern Beothuk people, had once done. He continued to wear the war paint afterward because he felt it gave him some sense of individuality among his peers.

Hayoka never felt at home among the Thrown-Aways. They had always sensed something odd about him. His late father's alliance with the hated Vykans did nothing to make Hayoka more acceptable to the rest of the Teketsertok. Some people worried that he might have inherited his father's tendency to betray his own tribe, just as Hobomok had betrayed the Itiwana. His insistence on wearing the Beothuk war paint, even during periods of peace, also marked him as different from the others. Hayoka didn't have many friends, and although people were cordial to him, no one except Nulia seemed too inclined to bond with him.

The eerie oddness that people detected in him was the spirit of the coyote, which had possessed his soul from the day his father died. Even before he was born, it dwelled inside him. All his life, he'd had this dark force within him, whispering to him. The voice told him that he was not like other men and had a special destiny. That voice frequently whispered the word "Itiwana" to him.

Hayoka had finally decided to ask his mother about the Itiwana, although he didn't tell her where he had heard the name. The Painted Woman told him that his father had once been the greatest hunter and warrior among the Itiwana. She claimed that he should rightfully have been named leader until he was killed by his own people in a power struggle. She reminded him that the Itiwana were the ones who had abandoned the people of Teketsertok to battle the Vykans alone.

Hayoka didn't quite know what to make of this news. On the one hand, the Itiwana were his people, but on the other hand, they had killed his father. Other people in the tribe seemed to have nothing good to say about the late Hobomok, although they were also less than staunch in their advocacy of the Itiwana.

Hayoka sought out Nulia for advice. She was his only real friend among the Thrown-Aways, and she also knew the Itiwana fairly well. Nulia explained to Hayoka that the Itiwana were not bad people, despite the decision their leader made. She maintained that Hobomok's fate was as much his own fault as it was the Itiwana's. Hayoka asked Nulia what she honestly thought about the Itiwana.

"The Itiwana disappointed me," she said. "They disappointed all of us. We joined them, thinking they were as committed to fighting our mutual enemy as we were. Sadly, it was not that way. They gave up their noble goal of defeating the Vykans, even after those barbaric fiends had killed the best man among them. His name was Pogum, and I loved him once when I was quite young. I had never met a finer man until I met Elder Brother. But Pogum was a great hero, and he was killed defending the Itiwana, and they did nothing. I cannot forgive them for that. But they are not evil. I don't quite know what else to say about them. Perhaps one day you will meet them and decide what kind of people they are for yourself."

Eventually, that was exactly what Hayoka decided to do. He knew he did not belong with the Thrown-Aways, and the voice in his head kept telling him his destiny was with the Itiwana. He made the decision to seek them out. It was almost as if he was being compelled to go to them.

The day he chose to leave Teketsertok, he sought out his mother, who was washing clothes by the lake. When he told her his plans, she reacted rather coldly. "There is nothing for you among those treacherous people. This is your home. It always has been."

Hayoka was adamant about his decision. "This has never been my home. From the day I was birthed, I have been unwelcomed here. They look at me as if I were a venomous snake slithering menacingly among them, just waiting for the proper moment to bite. I do not belong here."

The distraught Painted Woman tightened her grip as she squeezed the wet clothes. "And you believe that you belong with them? With the Itiwana?"

"I am not certain of anything, mother," Hayoka told her. "Except that my destiny lies elsewhere. This place holds nothing for me. I fully believe that I must spend some time among my father's people in order to understand who I am and what my purpose is."

His mother was more hurt than angry. "I do not understand you, boy."

"I do not understand myself sometimes, mother. I just know that I have been chosen for something greater."

The Painted Woman looked at the lake and saw a big fish eating a smaller one. "To leave a safe place and find your way among strangers is a difficult passage for anyone, my son. Especially if those strangers are enemies of your blood."

"I don't expect it to be easy," he said, splashing his foot in the water. "But I would like your blessing."

The Painted Woman refused to look at him, sulking. "I don't think you came here to discuss this. I think you came here to tell me that your mind is made up."

"You're correct."

"Then what should I say to you?" she said. "You've come to announce you're leaving me.

Leaving your home. What does my blessing matter? How shall I respond?"

"Forgive me for angering you, mother," he said, kneeling respectfully. "But I must go."

"When?" she said, looking at his reflection in the water.

"Now."

The Painted Woman still refused to look directly at him. "You won't even say goodbye to the rest?"

"Only Nulia," he said. "The rest can march off a cliff, and I would not care."

"Go then," she snapped in anger, roughly splashing the clothes in the lake. "Leave us. Go join your Itiwana kin."

"Don't be so distressed, mother," Hayoka said. "I won't be gone forever. I just want to visit Shipapa-Lina. Perhaps I will find I hate them. I may even wish them dead."

Pahana, Calian, and the twin brothers had left the Land of Everlasting Summer once again. They had been away from home for several days and had strayed farther than they had originally planned. However, Pahana was determined to find Lucifee the poshayanki Wildcat, and the thought of returning home without dragging the carcass of the wild beast behind him was anathema to him. As for O'Yewa and Masewa, they were just having fun and enjoying the adventure.

Calian was the only one among them who worried they might be needed back at Shipapa-Lina. He feared that Lucifee might be deliberately baiting the best Itiwana warriors away from home in order to weaken the tribe for an attack by Dagwona. Tawa had expected an attack, and Calian wanted to be with his people, defending their home. Still, it wasn't his place to question his clan elder-son and future leader of the Itiwana.

The four of them had been riding for hours when they came across a footprint. A large one. Calian leaped off his mount to study it more closely. He kneeled and ran his finger along the edge of the print.

"Is it what I believe it to be?" Pahana asked.

Calian nodded. "A Gichi-Awas print. A disconcertingly large one."

O'Yewa looked around. "Too big to be hiding in the bushes, I'd guess."

"True, this is," Masewa added. "And the stench of it would be assailing our noses were it still close."

"It wasn't too long ago that it passed here," Calian said. "It's likely not too far away. We were lucky to miss it."

"Why so?" O'Yewa asked. "Another potential adventure?"

"There aren't enough of us to bring such a beast to heel," Calian said. "We'd be witless to try."

"I'm willing, oh worrisome one," O'Yewa commented. "Who else feels witless?"

Pahana waved his hand to indicate his rejection of the idea. "You two would enjoy being mauled before breakfast, but unlike you, I have not forgotten why we're here. We're looking for Lucifee. The Gichi-Awas is a challenge and a menace, and as much as I'd love to march home with its huge head in my hands, we must not break our focus on the hunt for that damnable wildcat. I have foresworn myself to seeing Lucifee's teeth decorating father's wall."

"Then, you're decided?" Masewa asked.

"I am decided," Pahana said. "I want the wildcat. Come."

The foursome rode onward. Calian was concerned that they were still being led farther from the safety of home. *This is unwise,* he thought. *Something dangerous is waiting for us. We're going to regret not turning around and going home. This is the beginning of something unpleasant.*

CHAPTER FIVE

Hayoka sailed down the Endless River Agazzi on a log. With his feet in the water, he paddled with a hand-carved wooden paddle. He was getting sore in the rear, being straddled across the log for several days, but at least he was making good progress. As he traveled, he could feel the temperature rising each hour. He'd never been to the southern part of Ulah-Nane before now, and the closer he got to the Land of Everlasting Summer, the more he sweat. He knew this was due to the Tree of Life, which kept the cold away. He found himself savoring the warmth. He liked the hot weather so much that he tossed his fur cloak into the water.

So this is the Kisose... the long summer, he thought. *I quite like this.*

He altered his course, floating into the shallows. Hayoka waded to the shore for an evening rest. He lay on the warm grass near the river. It was as comfortable as his bed back in Teketsertok, but the ants became annoying. Despite the pests, he managed to fall asleep. In his dreams, the voice of the coyote spurred him on, urging him to continue his quest.

When Hayoka awoke, he needed to find some food. The voice in his head whispered to him and told him to walk west. Hayoka was continually befuddled by that mysterious voice, constantly chattering in the back of his mind. He often tried to ignore it, but the voice of the coyote was relentless. In fact, when the coyote really wanted something, that voice could exert a powerful influence on Hayoka. Today, the coyote wanted Hayoka to walk to the west, and Hayoka walked west.

After striding in the warm sun for some time, he heard something moving in the bushes. He could smell an animal odor. He put an arrow into his bow and listened intently to decipher where the sound was coming from.

Show yourself, he thought.

At that moment, Lucifee the Wildcat leaped into view, snarling savagely. Hayoka was surprised by the sight of the saber-toothed beast. The red, brown, and black beast was only three feet high, but five feet from nose to rump. Its fangs were almost six inches long, and its eyes shined

with an eerie yellow glow. Lucifee growled ferociously, inching menacingly toward Hayoka.

Hayoka aimed an arrow at the beast although
his hands shook because he had never seen such a
creature. Strangely though, that voice in his head
shouted urgently, ordering him not to shoot. The
voice insisted that Lucifee was not his enemy.
Hayoka hesitated, unsure of what to do.

Lucifee seemed equally unsure. The beast
paused as if it sensed something familiar about
the human. It studied the man who stood before
it. Lucifee appeared to recognize him, despite
never having seen this human before. Lucifee
crouched, poised to strike, but not moving.

Both Hayoka and Lucifee stared at each other,
neither advancing nor attacking. The strange
standoff lasted for several long, tense moments.
Finally, Lucifee moved close enough to get a good
sniff of the human and finally realized who he was
dealing with.

The wildcat cocked his head to the side.
"Kyyyyy-yoooooo-teeeeee."

Did that creature just call me Coyote? Hayoka
wondered. *And why do I feel like I've seen
it before?*

The strange meeting was interrupted when an
arrow hit Lucifee. The wildcat howled and raised
its hackles, scanning the area with all its senses.
Who would dare attack a poshayanki?

Lucifee saw Calian perched in a tree, placing a
second shaft in his bow and aiming. The wildcat

roared and charged toward the tree in a crazed rage. Hayoka could only watch in confused fear.

Calian fired two more shafts, which only served to anger the wildcat. Lucifee leaped onto the tree and began scampering up. Calian, always prepared, had a stone club in his possession and slammed it into the creature's nose.

Lucifee was stunned and fell from the tree. Back on the ground, the wildcat snarled furiously and prepared to leap upward again. The creature's attention was diverted from Calian when it heard the rumble of heavy hooves. From three separate directions came Pahana, O'Yewa, and Masewa, mounted atop World Giant, Lightning Charger, and Thunder Rumbler. They closed in on the wildcat rapidly.

The trio of bison sensed the presence of the creature which had been attacking them. The huge animals snorted with primal fury, running with the intention of destroying the wildcat utterly.

Lucifee realized the danger it was in. The wildcat had fought these divinely bred, extremely large bison and knew how formidable they were. Even fierce Achiyala feared these brutes. Lucifee tended to attack members of the herd in the dark, when they were isolated from the rest, gazing on their own. Sometimes Lucifee was able to get the better of them when taking advantage of a surprise attack. More often than not, however, the bison were able to drive the wildcat off. Now Lucifee was outnumbered three-to-one. There was no way even a poshayanki could take on three such large creatures, all mystically bred by the White Buffalo Woman. Lucifee made a desperate dash through the space between Lightning Charger and Thunder Rumbler.

Pahana was not going to let him get away that easily and shouted some taunts at the wildcat. "You are not staying, Lucifee? And after we have expended so much time bringing these tasty bison to you. Run if you will, because we love a good chase."

The three men and their bison chased Lucifee into the distance. Calian climbed down from the tree and retrieved his mount, Walking Storm, which was grazing some distance away. Calian noticed Hayoka still standing nearby and decided to investigate this stranger. From his vantage point, it seemed that Lucifee had spared the man. Why would a poshayanki—bred by the Sky Gods for battle and sworn to serve the Enemy Way—allow a human to live?

Hayoka's mind was whirling with bewilderment. Why did that cat-creature call him Coyote? Why didn't it attack him? And why did he feel like he knew the creature? There was something so familiar about that creature. Why was it so resistant to arrow wounds? It was baffling to him.

Leading his bison behind him by the reins, Calian approached Hayoka suspiciously. He suspected that the unknown man might be part of the Enemy Way. He held the club in his hand, prepared to swing it.

"Who are you?" Calian asked.

Hayoka was intimidated by the stone weapon wielded by a stranger. He remained calm, not wanting to antagonize the man. "My name is Hayoka of the Thrown-Away tribe of Teketsertok in Norumbega."

"I know of them," Calian said. "You're a long distance from home, I'd remark."

"I am; there's no dispute," Hayoka replied. "And who may you be?"

"Calian of the Itiwana of Shipapa-Lina in the Land of Everlasting Summer."

Hayoka's mood switched from scared to surprised. "You're of the Itiwana? All four of you?"

"We have that blessing, yes."

Hayoka could scarcely believe his incredible fortune. His wanderings had brought him directly to the very people he was looking for. In less than a week, he'd found the Itiwana. *The voice in my head led me to them.*

"You seem surprised, wanderer," Calian remarked.

"Yes, I supposed I am. I've ... heard of you."

Calian nodded. "Yes, we have a past connection to your Thrown-Aways. My father Pogum died fighting alongside them."

Hayoka knew the name well. Nulia had often told him about Pogum, who she once loved. "You're the son of Pogum?"

"You know of my father?" Calian asked, raising an eyebrow.

"His name is well spoken of among my people."

41

Calian was finding this all too coincidental. "You were very lucky today. That beast could have ripped you to pieces. I'm very surprised it did not. Why do you think it spared you?"

Hayoka wasn't sure of the answer to that question himself, and he wasn't prepared to discuss it with a stranger. "I fear I have no sensible explanation for that. I am as perplexed as you. I suppose the stars favored me today."

"Born under a fortunate star, were you?" Calian asked sarcastically.

"Not exactly," Hayoka replied.

The heavy hoof sounds of bison ended the conversation. Pahana and the twins rode into view. When they got closer, Hayoka could see they were not very happy. Calian apparently noticed it also.

"Lucifee eluded you, did he?" Calian asked.

Pahana glowered in embarrassed anger. "The cowardly creature fled faster than our mounts could pursue."

"Who could guess that the craven beast could run so fast?" Masewa said.

"Our mounts are mighty, but not spectacular in long-distance stamina," O'Yewa commented. "They tire easily during a chase. Lucifee does not have that difficulty."

Pahana shook his fist. "If only I'd been able to reach it. Should I ever catch that cowardly cat, I'll trample upon its leering face and sing a merry tune as I do so."

Calian gestured toward the northerner. "Your pardon, honored Pahana. This is Hayoka of the

Thrown-Away tribe of Teketsertok in Norumbega. Hayoka, this is Pahana, clan elder-son and heir of Shipapa-Lina. Those two are our kinsmen, Masewa and O'Yewa."

Hayoka bowed his head slightly. "It is an honor."

"What is a Thrown-Away doing so far south?" Pahana asked.

"Here lies a story," Hayoka said. "I came to find you, and fate brought you straight to me."

"Then join us and tell your story," Pahana said. "I could use an interesting tale just now. Come, we'll catch something to eat and camp for a meal, during which we'll tell tales of fate and beasts and brave men."

"You may ride with me," O'Yewa said.

"Many thanks for your graciousness," Hayoka replied.

The five men set off to hunt for their lunch, but Calian had a bad feeling about Hayoka. *My instincts tell me that this man has dark secrets.*

CHAPTER SIX

It was raining heavily in the Land of Everlasting Summer. Somber clouds and rumbling thunder lent a sense of dread to the air. Despite being a hearty group of people, most of the Itiwana chose to take shelter from the storm. It wasn't simply the inclement weather that they were concerned about. It was the feeling that there was more to this sudden downpour than normal nature. Everyone among the Itiwana seemed to sense it was a manifestation of something more sinister.

Tawa looked out the entrance of his cliff dwelling, seeing bolts of lightning striking the Shining Rock Mountains and the Hanging cliff above. The lightning almost seemed angry.

Pinga sat up in their feathered bed, seeing her husband's unease. "This One feels your pensiveness, dearest one."

Tawa rushed to her bedside, glad that she was awake. "Are you well, my sweet goddess?"

"This One has been worse," she said with a smile. "She will be perfectly well soon. But she can see your concern. She knows what troubles you."

"Are they fighting?" Tawa asked, looking out at the menacing skies. "Are the Sky Gods in combat above us? So savage. So powerful."

"It is difficult for This One to say, husband," Pinga answered. "She is no longer connected to the Sky Gods. Manabazo would know better than she does."

"I must ask him on the morrow," Tawa said.

"And when you do, ask him if he knows where our son is," Pinga insisted. "This One worries when he is away for so long. Our daughter safely studies with Molowia, but that boy and his companions can be so reckless."

"Pahana is a strong warrior, my love," Tawa answered. "Aholi has formidable sons as well. And wily Calian will look after them. That boy is as wise as Pogum himself was. He'll bring them home. Don't fear. But if it gives you comfort, I will surely ask Manabazo for his insight. I've no doubt he'll say they are frittering the hours away, hunting and telling stories."

Pahana, O'Yewa, Masewa, and Calian sat around the fire with Hayoka, eating the meat from their successful deer hunt. The deer and other large game had returned to the Land of Everlasting Summer in the years since Achiyala was driven away by Yana-Luha.

Three of the young Star Clan adventurers told stories about battles with the Tunerak Destroyer and the skinwalkers. Hayoka talked about battles with the Vykans. Four of them laughed as they boasted and bragged about their adventures. Only Calian was silent, watching Hayoka closely, unable to rid himself of the foreboding sense of danger that this man brought with him. He wondered why the others didn't feel it, too. Couldn't they see that this man was trouble?

Pahana seemed to be particularly enjoying Hayoka's company. "I wish I'd had the chance to fight those Vykan villains myself. My father defeated them once, before my mother created the truce between them and the Itiwana. We never got the chance to avenge my great-uncle Pogum. I regret I never got the opportunity to put arrows into those cold Vykan hearts."

Hayoka was glad this subject had been brought up. "The Thrown-Aways have a grudge against you for that. They feel that you, Itiwana, failed them by leaving my people alone to fight the Vykans. They feel you were selfish, so absorbed in your own affairs that you left the Thrown-Aways to resolve your troubles with the Vykans."

Calian pointed at Hayoka and raised his voice in defensive anger. "It was my father who defeated the Ice Wendigo Giwakna. If not for his heroism, Giwakna and his vile Vykans would have destroyed your Thrown-Aways long ago. My father sacrificed himself for both our tribes."

Hayoka held up his hands in a supplicating gesture. "Be at ease, my friend. I don't disagree. Pogum is hailed as a great hero among the Thrown-Aways. It is the rest of your tribe who are viewed as selfish and unreliable."

"Lies and nonsense," Pahana snapped indignantly. "My father had his reasons for doing what he did, and those reasons had nothing whatsoever to do with cowardice or selfishness or unreliability."

"Tawa is one of the greatest men to ever walk Ulah-Nane," Masewa snapped. "We will not hear him impugned. Do not speak further on it."

"Not unless you wish to learn how hard the warriors of the Star Clan can hit," O'Yewa added.

"Hold your anger, please," Hayoka said. "I was merely discussing what my people say about you. I, myself, have formed no opinion. I'm here to learn about you. I am part Itiwana."

"The son of a traitor," Calian stated.

"Enough tongue wagging," Pahana ordered, holding up a hand to indicate he wanted silence to speak. "Hayoka, you poor deluded man, you must be educated on the truth. If you want to learn more about us, then so you will. We will take you back to Shipapa-Lina, and you will see that my father is not what you have heard. I will introduce you to him so you can see the man he truly is, and then you can hear from his own tongue why he did what he did all those years ago."

Calian did not like this suggestion. He rose to his feet. "I advise against this idea, my clan elder-son. We have enough troubles to deal with in Shipapa-Lina without bringing the son of your father's old enemy to question him on something he did before any of us were born."

"You worry like a mother duck protecting her ducklings," Pahana said. "My decision is made. Hayoka, you will ride with me on World Giant. Come home with us to Shipapa-Lina."

"I will be honored, son of Tawa," Hayoka said with a slight bow.

Calian reluctantly held his tongue, although he knew this was a very poor idea. His senses were screaming that this newcomer would lead to no good.

Why won't he listen? Calian thought in frustration.

Hayoka was satisfied that this quest was leading exactly to the place he wanted to go and the people he wanted to meet. His moment of satisfaction was disturbed by the strange voice that came from nowhere. It spoke loudly and yet didn't seem to be a real voice at all.

"At last, I find you here, idle as a baby deer," the unseen speaker said.

The five young men looked up and saw an eagle perched on a tree branch. Except for Hayoka, they all knew who this speaking bird was.

"Manabazo," Pahana announced. "Has my father sent you to find us?"

"Your mother worries and wonders why you have tarried so long," Manabazo said. "As for your noble father, he knows that you are strong."

Hayoka's jaw dropped agape at the sight of the bird who spoke without actually speaking. What was this creature? Were such things common in the north?

I knew I'd see strange wonders once I left the Thrown-Aways, but I didn't anticipate this. Hayoka thought.

"Assure our mother that there is nothing to worry about," Pahana said. "We were merely enjoying the company of our new friend. We've yet to find Lucifee. When we do..."

Manabazo waved his wings for effect. "You will not do so this day because your good father orders you not to stay. Portents are appearing, and the day we feared may be nearing. Strong men are needed at home, and it's not the time to roam. Thus, if all talk is through, your new friend must excuse you. It's time to ride, to be at your honorable father and mother's side."

"If it is my father's will, we shall make haste," Pahana said.

"We shall not even remain to finish our meal," O'Yewa added.

"You show good sense," Manabazo said. "I will see you in three moons hence."

Manabazo flew off, leaving Hayoka flabbergasted. Pahana and the twins were disappointed their adventure was at an end. Calian was still concerned about Hayoka joining them.

This will not end well for us, he thought. As the others retrieved their mounts, Calian walked behind, feeling as if he had just seen the first part of the sky fall, and knew the rest of it would soon be falling as well.

"That was quite wonderful," Atira said, laying on her bed of hay and animal skins.

T'Soona, who lay next to Atira in her cave chamber on the cliffs, stretched and grinned in sensual satisfaction. "Why should today be any different?"

She turned on her side and stroked his chest. "You've helped me take my mind off war and witches and the irresponsible behavior of my foolish grandson."

"You should not let worry consume you so much," he said, kissing her shoulder. "I never do."

"Indeed." She laughed. "And I adore that about you. You always lighten my moods. Either by words or by ... other things."

"Sweet Atira," he said, taking her hand. "Something else that might brighten your spirit and distract you from your troubles is..."

"Don't!" she retorted, sitting up. "Don't ask me that again."

T'Soona hid his disappointment under a mask of mirth. "I was just going to ask if you would like to learn to juggle. I'm rather good at it."

She gazed at him tenderly, touching his hair. "I do cherish you and the time we have together, my sweet T'Soona. You make my life better and happier. But I will never love anyone except Yana-Luha. I will never be the wife of anyone other than Yana-Luha."

T'Soona got to his feet and began to put on his garments. "There are important things we should be doing. Gods and witches won't stop their plots and plans out of respect for our primal urges."

"You're hurt," she said sadly.

He put on his moccasins. "I'm always happy. Ask anyone. T'Soona is always jesting."

She stood up, wrapping a wolf pelt around herself. "My poor, dear T'Soona. You should stop waiting for me. As much as it would hurt my heart, you should find a woman of your own. I feel very guilty that you've spent too many years hoping for me to change my answer."

T'Soona walked to the cave mouth. "I have no choice. I will never love anyone except Atira. I will never have a wife except Atira. That is my stubborn decision. Nothing either of us can do will change it. Please excuse me. I must attend to some people who are feeling poorly."

He slipped out of the cave chamber, and Atira's shoulders slumped. *I hate hurting him. He's the*

*kindest, gentlest man I've ever met. In other cir-
cumstances, I could easily fall in love with him.
But we need to accept the harsh reality we live in.
All of us. Life in Shipapa-Lina often seems cursed.
I wonder how my granddaughter is managing
in Kolhu.*

The Sun Dagger House of the community of
Kolhu was the largest, most majestic of the Great
Houses of the impressive city. Four levels high,
with hundreds of rooms and several kivas, it was
the heart of the community. Kolhu was the most
advanced and modern city in Ulah-Nane.

Molowia, the Cacique Shaman Chief of Kolhu
and aunt of Tawa, walked pensively through the
Sun Dagger House. Short and stout with graying
hair, she had seen over 50 summers. Molowia
had ruled Kolhu for more than thirty summers.
The war of the Sky Elders, while currently quiet,
weighed heavily on her. Her shamanic senses
had sensed the recent attack by the Witch of the
Whirlwind, and she'd had a premonition that
worse danger was on the horizon. She had managed to keep Kolhu from getting directly involved
in the war for years. She did not want her people to
be caught in a war they had no stake in. However,
she did not know how long she could continue to
keep the Itiwana of Kolhu safe.

She walked into the Cacique chamber, where
she oversaw the government of Kolhu. Inside was

her disciple Kia, the daughter of Tawa and Pinga. Tawa was Molowia's nephew. Kia was a petite girl of fourteen summers. Unlike her brother, Pahana, who had snow-white skin and ebony hair, Kia had bronzed skin with silvery-white hair and eyes.

Kia, who was a mastop-kachina like the rest of her family, had displayed extra-sensory cognitive abilities at an early age. Pinga felt that Molowia, the powerful shaman, would be the best person to train her in the use of her developing capabilities. Since Pahana was destined to be the next kik-mongwi of Shipapa-Lina, and Molowia had no heir, it was agreed that Kia would go to live in Kolhu. The child was training not only to be a shaman but also to rule Kolhu one day.

Kia was currently levitating several inches above her feathered seat. Around her was a swarm of flies, circling her body like the rings of Saturn. With her eyes closed, she somehow directed the swarm to orbit around her faster and faster, their buzz increasing.

Molowia watched the girl for a few seconds, nodding with satisfaction at the speed at which she was learning. *Impressive, indeed.*

"Well done, child," Molowia said aloud.

Startled, Kia lost concentration, causing the flies to disperse and herself to fall. "Ow!"

Molowia chuckled. "Control, child. Always maintain control. And you must be aware of your surroundings. You should have sensed me coming, even with your eyes closed."

"I am sorry, Cacique," Kia said. "I will do better."

Molowia sat down on a seat of hay, swatting away flies. "Controlling insects is a rare and difficult talent. Few shamans ever manage it. Even I have great difficulty with it. Your level of mastery of these tiny creatures is extraordinary. It must be your combined heritage as the child of a mastop-kachina and a quondam Sky Elder. Who can be sure of the limits of your power?"

"I am excited to learn how powerful I am, Cacique," Kia replied.

Molowia held up a warning finger. "It is not about power, child! It is about control and responsibility. Gaining too much power before you are mature enough to handle your abilities can lead to your soul becoming corrupted. Your gifts are to be used for the good of the Itiwana. You serve, even when you rule."

Kia lowered her gaze. "I'm sorry."

Molowia hated to scold Kia. The young girl had gained such a hold on her heart it was sometimes difficult to be firm with her. But Molowia knew she had to impose discipline at a young age, because the temptation of power was strong for one so young. Kia, more than other children, needed to learn discipline and control.

"We'll try something else now," Molowia said. "But first, get rid of these flies."

CHAPTER SEVEN

Tawa was upset because there was nothing for him to do at the moment. The signs and omens were pointing toward something unpleasant on the horizon, and Manabazo had confirmed that the recent storms were caused by the Sky Elders battling above, unseen, but not without being noticed. Tawa wanted to do something to ensure that his people were safe, but he did not know what he could do. Other than the usual ritual of keeping his people well-trained and remaining constantly vigilant, there was nothing else to be done. He fervently wished he could do more. He hated the waiting.

Tawa walked to the bison pen, where Ashiwi, the beast master, was tending to Mountain Fury.

The old bison had taken a beating from the battering cyclone winds. The animal had stood its ground valiantly, but this latest battle had taken its toll. Tawa noticed that Mountain Fury had moved slowly and gingerly while trotting back to the village after the Whirlwind Witch's assault. Tawa had left his steed in the care of Ashiwi, who knew more about the treatment of bison than anyone else.

Ashiwi was feeding some sort of plant herbs to Mountain Fury when Tawa arrived. The animal reacted to its master's presence, raising its head and grunting. Tawa patted the big bison.

"Hello, boy," Tawa said. "How are you, large one?"

"He's old," Ashiwi said. "Despite his impressive size and power, he does not have the stamina he once had. He has pain in his back legs and tires easily. I regret to say I fear his days as a battle steed are behind him."

Tawa gently put a hand on his steed's head. "I understand. I've been thinking the same thing. He's served me so well for so many years. I was loath to part with him. He saved my life when Stone Coat was ready to slay me. He's been a wonderful friend, but it would be cruel to force him to continue his duty in his final years. He's earned a rest."

Slowly, Tawa unhooked the saddle and harness from Mountain Fury. He took the big beast by the horn and led it away. "Come along, old friend. It's time you enjoyed some well-deserved peace."

With a funereal pace, Tawa led Mountain Fury down the Mesa and onto a grassy field known as Teshkiwi. It was a quiet area between the outer farms and the rooster pens. Old Pekwin used to meditate there, and sometimes Manabazo would use the field to commune with his fellow Sky Elders. Aside from the roosters and rabbits, there were three young, white bison wandering the fields. White bison were sacred, and they were set free rather than being used for battle or food.

"Here we are, boy," Tawa said, making a wide gesture toward the field. "Here's your new home. These young albinos will keep you company."

Mountain Fury stood uncomprehendingly. Tawa began petting his snout, comforting the bison. "I will miss having you with me in battle, old friend. It was always a comfort to have your power beneath me. No man ever had a finer steed than Mountain Fury. You were magnificent."

He swatted Mountain Fury on the rump. "Go now. Make friends with the young ones. Enjoy your rest."

Mountain Fury took a few steps forward, then stopped, looking back at Tawa. He was confused. The animal was still clearly loyal to his master.

"Go on, boy," Tawa said. "I'll come back to visit you often. We'll take long walks in the woods, and I'll bring you fine, tasty treats. We will always be friends. I shall miss you. Now go."

Mountain Fury trotted forward and stopped again. Tawa turned away with a lump in his throat. He looked back to see Mountain Fury following him and gestured for the loyal steed to stop. "Stay, boy. Stay."

Tawa walked away while the confused Mountain Fury snorted, upset at being left behind. "Go be happy, Mountain Fury. Go and run free."

The three young, white bison came closer to Mountain Fury, circling and sniffing him. The bison studied each other, beginning the process of accepting Mountain Fury into their group. Tawa left the field, confident that Mountain Fury would bond with his new herd. He was surprised by how sad he was at leaving his mount behind.

After the sad separation with Mountain Fury, Tawa spent the bulk of the day performing his usual duties as kik-mongwi, wherein he settled some minor disputes and observed Aholi drilling his braves. He could not ease the pensiveness and anxiety that filled him. Tawa chose to return to the Great Lodge of Shipapa-Lina and attempted to sleep. After lying down for a time, lost in his worries, he finally fell asleep.

At first, his dreams were pleasant, revisiting a day long ago when his son was young. He recalled taking Pahana and the twin sons of Aholi on a fishing trip. Suddenly, however, his sweet dreams were usurped by an outside force.

He found himself back in the crystal cave of the winds, where he'd met the Na-Ash-Jai Spider Women. In the dream, he was the same age as he had been that day. He knew this wasn't really a dream, yet he had no sense of danger. What was happening?

And then he saw them. As before, the Na-Ash-Jai Spider Women climbed out of the darkness.

"Greetings, Tawa of the Itiwana," Oona, the eldest, said. "It has been..."

"...many years," the youngest one, Abit, continued. "At least, it is long by..."

"...your reckoning," Echigas, the middle one, said. "To us, the intervening years have..."

"...been the blink of an eye," Oona added. "We have given you enough time."

"Time for what?" A confused Tawa asked.

"To repay your debt," Oona said. "Surely you have not forgotten..."

"...your vow to us," Echigas continued. "You swore..."

"...to do us a service at a time of our choosing," Abit said.

Tawa had genuinely forgotten. He had been a boy of 17 when he made that promise. It seemed longer than an eternity ago. Still, as he did make the vow and as a man of honor, he was bound to repay his debt. Aside from that, it would not be wise to antagonize three fierce-looking spider women. Who could be sure what they were capable of?

"I remember making that promise," Tawa said. "And I will not dishonor myself or my family or my tribe by breaking the oath. What would have me do?"

"We need to see better," Oona said. "Matters are coming quickly to a deadly collision, and yet..."

"...we cannot see the end of things," Echigas, continued. "We are the Eyes of the Future, but we cannot see how events will end. We also need to know..."

"...how to protect ourselves," Abit said. "We wish to survive the coming clash, and we need information in order to ensure our survival. Therefore..."

"...we need to see better," Oona announced.

"How can I help you with this?" Tawa asked.

Oona spoke. "You must retrieve for us a piece of Sanopi, the demon of mud, tar, and pitch, so that we can..."

"...complete the web of fate. Without an aspect of Sanopi..."

"...we remain in the dark and vulnerable."

Tawa was stunned by the request. "I've heard of this Sanopi creature from Manabazo. It is one of the Shiwana spirits. It is made of black ooze and goo. Such a creature would be hard to kill. Can even the Dragonfly kill a man of mud?"

"Your spear, as powerful as it is, will be useless. As you say,..."

"...a spirit of mud and glue and tar cannot be slain by a spear. You will need..."

"...another weapon."

Tawa was curious about this weapon. "What could that be?"

"Ask your albino spouse," Oona said. "She was once a..."

"...Sky God herself, and she still..."

"...has knowledge that can help you," Abit added.

Tawa nodded. "If you can't be any more helpful, then I will surely ask my wife. She will definitely make more of an effort to be useful."

"When you slay Sanopi for us, you must..."

"...trap his remains in a wooden case blessed by a shaman and lined with leaves and bark from Yaxche. Then..."

"...bring the box to us immediately so that we can complete the web of fate."

"I will."

"And now...

"...you may..."

"...awake."

Tawa's eyes opened, and he sat up in bed. He knew what he had experienced was not a dream. He knew what he had to do. Tawa woke his wife. "Pinga, I need you."

She slowly opened her eyes and looked at him groggily. "Now?"

"Wake up. I need your assistance. Now."

Pinga sat up. "Are you ill?"

"What I am is infuriated," Tawa said. "Furious that I can't escape my obligations, even in my dreams."

"What in Awona'Wilona's mighty name are you talking about?"

Tawa explained the vision and the debt he owed to the Na-Ash-Jai Spider Women. He mentioned Sanopi and what the Spider Women said about Pinga knowing how to kill it. Pinga listened, and despite her snow-white skin, Tawa thought she suddenly became pale.

"Do you know where I can find this creature and how I can destroy it?" he queried. "I hope you can be more informative than those damnable multi-legged web women. You'd think they'd be more helpful. Can you be?"

Pinga averted her eyes. "Such bad news. Sad news. This One wishes she were only dreaming this conversation. Why did you never tell This One of your debt to the Na-Ash-Jai?"

"It was a child's folly, long since forgotten," Tawa said. "At the time, it seemed necessary."

"This One wishes she had known of this, so she could have found a way to free you from this dread obligation," Pinga told him with concern. "It is never fortuitous to be in the debt of the Spider Women. This task proves it. This One fears for you."

"Specify, my dear wife. What are you afraid of, and what is the reason for this fear?"

Pinga sat hugging her knees. "The only way to kill Sanopi is with the Golden Arrow of Awona'Wilona, the one hidden by Cho-Chi-No years ago after your ancestor Morning Star used it to slay the fierce Shakok."

"I know that particular legend in detail," Tawa said. "Do you know where I can find the arrow?"

"This One does know, and it is the cause of her trepidation," Pinga told him. "It is in the north, in Nuremgard in Norumbega. It is in a cave guarded by a poshayanki called Nanook. He is called the Bear God by the Vykans."

"A poshayanki?" Tawa asked with a touch of dread. "Like A'Chiyala? The thing that took my father from me?"

"Indeed, so," she answered. "You've seen how powerful the Poshayanki are. You already lost your father to one of them. This One fears losing you to another. The Poshayanki are not to be underestimated. They are the war beasts of the Sky Elders, and they do not die easily."

Tawa nodded. "I'm well aware of what the poshayanki are capable of. It's one of the most vivid recollections of my life. Every nightmare I've ever had has included A'Chiyala. I will recall that experience until I stop breathing."

"And do you not fear?"

"Of course," Tawa answered. "But a chieftain should be afraid, because the fear makes a man alert. Yet it does not rule me... I rule the fear. I will not make my decisions out of fear, nor will I miss a chance to avenge my family's honor by destroying one of those disgusting poshayanki. And aside from that, I made a vow, and a kik-mongwi does not break vows."

Pinga was becoming more horrified with each second. "You must not, my love. This One cannot lose you. She lives for your embrace. She cannot stand the thought of your death."

Tawa caressed her gently. "And I savor your love. I savor your wisdom and your beauty. They inspire me. That is why I will fight my way back from any threat, even a poshayanki, to reach you again. And don't forget, I have the Dragonfly.

According to Manabazo, it can kill even a poshayanki."

Pinga nodded slightly. "This One knows that to be true. The Dragonfly is a great weapon. However, This One still fears for your safety. Down to her soul, she does."

"Don't fear for me," Tawa said to her reassuringly. "I have fought my way through dangers of every type since I was a mere boy. Sometimes I win, and sometimes I only survive, but I always return. It is my fate to lead the Itiwana through the war of the Sky Gods, and I intend to be here to do just that. The poshayanki will not have the last word. I will. I am the chieftain."

Despite her fears, Pinga had to smile. "What is it about the foolish courage of mortals that This One finds so appealing? Your bravery won her love years ago, and it still draws her to you like an insect to a flame. This One loves you, Tawa. Even if the world collapses and burns, she swears that this will always be true."

"And when the end comes, my last thoughts shall be of you."

Tawa and Pinga made love that night and forgot that the rest of the world existed. For that one night, Tawa forgot his destiny and allowed his wife's body to become his whole universe for a few hours.

It would be the last pleasant night he would ever have.

CHAPTER EIGHT

A fter days of travel, Pahana and his hunting party returned to Shipapa-Lina. The clan elder-son led the way upon World Giant, with Hayoka sitting behind him. O'Yewa and Masewa followed closely behind, bickering like oversized children. Calian brought up the rear on Walking Storm. Calian still was not happy about Hayoka's presence, but he'd been unable to change Pahana's mind.

Hayoka looked around in wonder. He'd heard rumors of the amazing cliff housing being built on the mountainside. He had been told by Pahana about their massive herds of huge bison. But what really impressed him was the Great Cliff Palace of Shipapa-Lina. He'd never seen a structure like it.

Remarkable, Hayoka thought. *These Itiwana are far ahead of the Thrown-Aways.*

O'Yewa and Masewa unleashed a chanting cry to announce their presence. Many people greeted the returning warrior foursome. A few young Itiwana lads rushed to take charge of their mounts and return them to the pens.

Pahana put a hand across Hayoka's shoulder and made a sweeping gesture. "Welcome to Shipapa-Lina, my friend."

"I stand impressed," Hayoka said. "How long did it take to build all this?"

"I see a hungry mind, eager to eat up knowledge," Pahana said. "My family built it after the last Sky Gods war, and we still defend it today."

Apparently, for the comfort of untrustworthy sons of traitors, Calian thought.

Atira spotted her newly returned kin and crossed the village clearing to meet them. "Ah, the wild warriors return to save the Itiwana from ennui."

"Pleasant morning, grandmother," Pahana said.

The twins made their greetings almost in unison, as they often did. They looked at each other in annoyance, as if each blamed the other for continually mimicking him.

"Pleasant morning," Calian said.

Atira was not smiling. "Where have you four fools been?"

Pahana was surprised. "Not the greeting I had expected. Your tone is decidedly hostile. What's angering you, grandmother?"

"Go see your parents immediately, boy," Atira said. "You've missed events you should not have missed."

Pahana began to wonder what had occurred. Many scenarios ran through his head. "I will do so."

Atira motioned toward Hayoka. "And who is this young man you've brought to us?"

"You will never guess," Masewa said.

"That much is certain," O'Yewa added.

Pahana put a hand on Hayoka's shoulder. "Grandmother, this man will be visiting with us for a time. He is actually one of us. He is Hayoka, the son of Hobomok, the hunter."

Atira's eyes flashed with cold anger when she heard the name of the traitor. "You are the son of Hobomok?" She asked, almost as an accusation.

"I understand that he is not well regarded among you," Hayoka said.

She looked sharply at Pahana. "What is this person doing in Shipapa-Lina, son?"

A fair question, Calian thought.

"He has questions to ask," Pahana said. "And it is time he had them answered. I think he should speak to my father."

"Your father has many other things on his mind at present," she answered, still watching Hayoka suspiciously. "This is no time to distract him with the son of..." she began, but stopped herself diplomatically.

"Traitors?" Hayoka asked.

"I did not like to use the word," Atira said. "But I knew your father well. I was here when he led the Vykans into our home. He was never an honorable man."

"I never met the man myself," Hayoka responded calmly. "But my mother had a different view of him. I'd like to learn the truth."

"Your grandmother is correct, my clan elder-son," Calian said. "Perhaps he should return some other day."

Pahana glared at Calian to be quiet. "I'm embarrassed by the two of you. This man is my guest and an Itiwana by blood. He is not guilty of his father's crimes. We will not send him away so abruptly. We will give him the opportunity to meet the man who his mother has defamed for so long, and he will see that the man who killed his father is not a monster or a villain but rather the greatest hero in Ulah-Nane."

"That he is," Atira replied. "I see that you are determined in this. I advise against it, but I will not argue this point at the moment. Your father is waiting for you. Hurry home."

"I will do as you say, grandmother," Pahana said. "Come along, Hayoka. Let's meet my father."

Pahana led Hayoka to the grand Cliff Palace, which impressed him at first sight. The largest of all the dwellings of Shipapa-Lina's cliff dwellings, the four-story palace housed 150 individual rooms, including twenty ceremonial kivas. The palace had a circular tower which served as the meeting site for the Shakowin council.

Pahana led Hayoka through the amazing structure made of sandstone, shale, mortar, and wooden beams. Strolling through the seemingly endless walkways, past the court and the main plaza, Hayoka was astounded, never having been inside such a towering edifice before. *These people are surprisingly advanced*, Hayoka thought.

They made their way up the stairs to the tower and found Tawa seated in the chieftain's place of honor. It was a small stool carved from a log, adorned with images of sacred animal spirits. On one side of him, the Dragonfly was sticking out of the ground, and in front of him was a fire pit. Tawa seemed to be in deep meditation. Pahana knew his father only did this when he was preparing for something important and dangerous.

"Father?"

Tawa glanced askew at his son, with a cold expression. Tawa rose and glared at the two arrivals. Ignoring the stranger, he crossed the chamber to meet Pahana and abruptly slapped his son across the face.

Hayoka did not know what was going on but deduced that he had come at a bad time. He stepped back discretely into the entranceway to the Shakowin chamber.

Pahana rubbed his sore cheek, stunned by the slap. "I don't understand, father."

"What grave sin have I committed to have sired such an irresponsible fool?" Tawa chided loudly. "Were you asleep when I informed you that we were expecting the Witch of the Whirlwind to attack within the upcoming days? And were you still slumbering when I enlightened you that your natural-born ability was our best defense? I can only assume that you napped through all such talk; otherwise, you would not have wandered off when you were needed here."

Pahana began to realize what had happened. "Did the witch attack while I was gone?"

Tawa folded his arms. "Your brain is beginning to work, I see. Far too late, but an encouraging sign, just the same. Yes, she attacked as predicted. And had it not been for the actions of your courageous mother, she would have done immense damage to Shipapa-Lina."

"Mother drove the villain away?" Pahana asked.

"She did," Tawa said as he pointed accusingly at his son. "And she paid dearly for it. She was ill for days. Only now is she back on her feet, albeit still weak. You know she can no longer safely utilize such power, having been banished from the kinship of her fellow Sky Elders. The strain nearly killed her."

Pahana's heart sank with guilt. "I'm sorry, father. I am indeed a fool. I believed I could kill the wildcat and return before the witch made her appearance. It was stupid of me."

"We can agree on that," Tawa said. "Did you at least catch your wildcat?"

"I regret to say no," Pahana replied, embarrassed. "We came close, but he fled too quickly."

"A perfect failure all around," Tawa said, pacing around the chamber. "Still, there's one positive aspect. It's fortunate that you've returned before

I was forced to depart. I wasn't sure you would. You walk your own way of late."

"But where are you going, father?"

Tawa looked down at the burned embers in the fire pit. "I need to settle an old debt, son. I must travel up north to Norumbega. Your mother will explain the details. I expect I shall be gone for several cycles of the full moon. I had hoped you would lead in my absence, but you've caused me to doubt you."

Pahana kneeled in front of his father. "Don't dismiss me so abruptly, father. I made a mistake, but I am humbled by it. I have learned and I will not fail the Itiwana again."

Tawa put a hand on his son's shoulder. "Perhaps I am blinded by my affection for you, but I will give you a chance to prove yourself. Still, I shall appoint your grandmother as your advisor and overseer. If she decides you are not worthy of the task I have assigned you, she will be permitted to replace you until I return. Her judgment is rarely erroneous."

"If that is your will father, I accept your decision," Pahana said. "I will not disappoint you again."

"We shall see," Tawa said. "But you've brought a visitor, haven't you?"

Tawa approached Hayoka to inspect him more closely. "So calm and yet so pensive. He looks almost familiar. Do I know your people, young one?"

"I am Hayoka, son of Hobomok the Hunter, who was born here in Shipapa-Lina," Hayoka responded, wondering if his identification would be taken as badly by Tawa as it was with his mother.

"Of course, I should have recognized you immediately," Tawa said. "But I confess I hadn't thought of your father lately. I've had other matters to distract me. So, the son of Hobomok has come to the Itiwana, has he? I thought I was done with your family line. But the past never seems to stay dead, does it? Have you come here with anger in your heart, son of Hobomok? Or is there something else on your mind?"

"I have questions, great Kik-Mongwi," Hayoka said, trying to sound as respectful as possible. "Questions about my father and why he did what he did and why you killed him. There is a lot I wish to know about the man who died before I was born."

"Excellent questions, and I don't blame you for asking them," Tawa said. "Of course, some questions are best unasked and unanswered, but nevertheless, I respect your questioning spirit. Look at you... so curious. Years of wondering should be quelled with the truth."

"You will answer my questions, then?" Hayoka asked.

Tawa pulled Dragonfly from the ground, which made Hayoka quite nervous. "It's a lonely way, the way of a chieftain. We often have to do things that others would not understand. We have a unique vision of the world. When you become a chieftain, you become an entirely new person, and the old one dies. Have you ever been a chieftain, Hayoka?"

"No, kik-mongwi."

"Then do not hope to completely understand me," Tawa said, staring at the Dragonfly. "I will answer your questions when I return, but I suspect you will not fully grasp the colossal ramifications and the intricate web of fate being woven."

"I will try to understand as best I can, Kik-Mongwi," Hayoka replied.

"Very well then," Tawa said. "We will talk when I return. I do not promise that you will be invited to stay in Shipapa-Lina after our conversation, but for the moment, you may remain as Pahana's guest."

Pahana grinned and bowed slightly. "Thank you, father."

Tawa put his hand on his son's head. "It is time for me to walk my own way. I leave Shipapa-Lina in your care, my son. Look to the Shakowin for guidance. Your mother and your grandmother will not lead you astray. Manabazo is a storm of wisdom. Remember, there are others more experienced here than yourself. Don't be headstrong. Be a leader."

"I will, father."

"And now I must go," Tawa said. "I wish to say goodbye to others before I depart."

Tawa left the room and Pahana followed behind him. Hayoka stood alone in the Shakowin chamber. He could not help thinking that all this could have been his, if his father had become chieftain instead of being exiled and later killed. He wondered if fate had the same thing in store for him. Or, perhaps, he may one day have to do what he told his mother he would do and make the Itiwana pay for their past actions. *It will be up to the great Sky Elders to decide if I am among friends or enemies. Have I found a new home, or has fate brought me here to be a deadly avenger?*

CHAPTER NINE

I *will need to leave my home today*, Tawa thought on the morning of his journey. He spent several hours after dawn riding upon a young bison called Brave Fire. The animal was the spawn of Mountain Fury and had been trained by Ashiwi as a replacement for Mountain Fury. Ashiwi knew months ago that Mountain Fury's advanced age would necessitate the appointing of a new steed for the kik-mongwi and had been preparing Brave Fire for the role. Tawa had ridden him before and now was spending the morning bonding with his new mount.

I suppose I can't delay any longer, he thought. *Time to go.*

Tawa said his goodbyes to his family, particularly Pinga. Alone in their cave, he wiped a tear from her eyes.

"You will not change your mind, my love?" she asked.

"You know my answer," he said. "Sometimes we must leave our safe places and walk empty-handed among our enemies. No more tears. Every quest must begin with goodbye. Knowing you'll be here waiting for me will be my greatest inspiration to succeed. Now close your eyes and sing that ancient melody you like to sing. And when you open your eyes, I will be gone."

"Yes, my Tawa," she said and began to sing. Tawa silently backed out of the chamber, looking lovingly at his wife. He heard her singing as he descended the cliff housing.

Tawa left final instructions for Pahana regarding how to handle his tenure as acting chieftain of the Itiwana. He also checked in with the members of the Shakowin to remind them that they needed to be supportive of the young clan elder-son, but also be sufficiently adamant about pointing out any mistakes he might make while Tawa was gone. Atira didn't need to be reminded of that. She was always quick to chastise the boy when he was wrong. Atira promised she would oversee Pahana's rule and make sure the boy was wise.

The entire village turned out to give the exalted kik-mongwi a respectful sendoff. A ritual "good luck" dance was done, and flowers were placed along the path for their leader to ride over. Tawa thanked his people for their warm send-off and promised to come back. "You will see me again," he announced. "I was born in Shipapa-Lina and I will always return."

Before he left, he took his cousin Calian aside. "A word in your ear, cousin."

"My ear is always yours, kik-mongwi."

They moved where others could not hear them. "Good Calian. Wise Calian. Outside of the members of the Shakowin, you are the wisest man in Shipapa-Lina. We all acknowledge this. Did you know that? Despite your youth, you impress everyone with your sage mind. You seem to have inherited your father's wisdom."

"Thank you, kik-mongwi. You honor me."

"I need you to use that swift, observant mind and fine instincts in order to act as my ears and eyes while I am away," Tawa said. "I detect that you have the same reservations I do regarding our unexpected guest. I have no time to deal with this matter here and now. Until I return, it will comfort me immensely to know that you are keeping a watchful eye on this Hayoka. Pahana is strong, and he's brave, and he's a great warrior, but he is too confident for someone so young. He still allows his pride to rule him at times. He is much as I was before my father left us. Also, he seems too trustful of his new friend. I've taught him much, but he still has more to learn. Until he does, his advisors and our clan will have to do what time has not yet done for him."

"I understand."

"I know you do," Tawa said. "Be watchful. Be alert. Mark well and remember. Whatever perfidy you may notice, inform the Shakowin immediately. Not Pahana, but the Shakowin only. Confide in my mother. You must be vigilant, above all. If you are lax in this, you may be the ruin of our tribe. Don't fail me."

"I swear on my father's noble soul that I will never relax my vigil, Kik-Mongwi."

"Excellent, Calian. And now it's time for me to go."

Tawa climbed upon Brave Fire, securing his provisions and his precious Dragonfly to the mount with some woven netting. He looked around and saw Pinga standing outside the Great Lodge, looking disconsolate. She blew a parting kiss to him. He nodded reassuringly, as if making a promise to return.

Tawa nudged Brave Fire, who trotted forward. O'Yewa and Masewa joined a few other young Itiwana in pounding out a steady drumbeat to accompany their leader's departure. Tawa waved goodbye and rode out of Shipapa-Lina on his quest of honor. There was a profound sense of trepidation as he left because many of the Itiwana feared that without his sage leadership, the Itiwana would be vulnerable to further attacks from the Tunerak Destroyers or the skinwalkers, or the witch herself. No one was sadder than Pinga, but she concealed herself inside the Great Lodge before she allowed herself to sob.

She didn't want anyone to notice her despondency. She needed to be seen as a strong, confident member of the Shakowin while her husband was gone. She prayed to Awona'Wilona that he would return.

Visualizing the spirit realm was a difficult and dangerous thing, even for an experienced shaman. For someone as youthful as Kia, it would seem a nearly impossible feat. Molowia had warned Kia not to do so. She insisted that Kia was too young and inexperienced to understand the perils inherent in the higher realms. Kia didn't agree with this, and Molowia would only say that she would explain it better when Kia was older and more seasoned.

That vague explanation never satisfied the young girl, who was becoming increasingly confident in her rapidly growing abilities. Kia was a prodigy and felt that Molowia was underestimating her power. *I am better than what she sees in me.*

Sitting in front of an open blue flame that flickered across the ceremonial kiva of the Sun Dagger house, young Kia stared fixedly into the crackling fire. Something about the raw, natural, elemental power of flame made it easier to pierce the harsh shroud of reality and see beyond the physical domain.

And the things she saw fascinated and thrilled her. Indescribable visions and unfathomable sounds assailed her senses, baffling her young mind. Kia couldn't comprehend most of what she was seeing, but it excited her more than anything she had ever experienced. *Incredible!*

And then she heard the voice...

"Well done, Kia. Well done," vocalized the mysterious consciousness. "Your power impresses. It impresses."

Kia gasped in alarm, looking around to see if there was someone else in the kiva. Confirming she was alone, she nervously turned her focus back to the strange ether realm she observed within the elemental flame. "Who spoke?"

The enigmatic voice replied, "Don't be alarmed. Don't be. I'm a friend. A friend."

Kia was unnerved by the mystery voice. "Who are you?"

"I'm Shula-Witsa. Shula-Witsa," said the voice.

It took Kia a moment to place the name. She had been taught about the Sky Elders, but there were so many, she had to root through her brain to recognize it. "The Fire Elder?"

"I am indeed. I am," the unseen Elder replied. "You interest me. You do."

"What do you mean?" Kia asked.

"You have power. You have," the Fire Elder said. "Such great power. Great power."

Kia was complimented by the praise of a divine being. "Thank you, great Elder."

"It is true. It is," Shula-Witsa said. "We've noticed you. We have."

She was both flattered and confused. "What do you want of me?"

"You can help. You can," the Elder said. "We Elders struggle. We struggle. There's a war. There is. We need allies. We do. You can help. You can."

"Me?" she said. "Wouldn't you rather have Molowia?"

"We would not. We wouldn't," the Fire Elder said. "She won't help. She won't. Kolhu is neutral. It's neutral. She disrespects us. She's disrespectful. She refuses us. She refuses."

"I know this," Kia said. She had always wondered about Molowia's staunch unwillingness to get involved in the war of the Sky Elders. The Tree of Life is important to everyone. It seemed unfair to let Shipapa-Lina carry the burden alone.

"You're so powerful. Quite powerful," Shula-Witsa said. "We need you. Need you. Molowia won't approve. She won't. But please help. Please help."

Kia hesitated. The great Sky Elders were personally asking her for assistance. She had a chance to help her parents in Shipapa-Lina. She had an opportunity to be as useful as her brother. And yet, Molowia had ordered her not to involve herself in this. How could she disobey her teacher?

"I... I need to think," Kia said.

"Think it over. Think well," the Fire Elder said. "We need you. Need you. I will return. I will."

The flame flickered, and the voice faded. Kia could no longer sense the presence of another. She was alone. But she still had a serious decision to make. Should she reject the Sky Elders and pass up a chance to help her tribe or should she defy Molowia?

Several weeks had gone by since Tawa had left Shipapa-Lina. Nothing of note had happened during that time, and some of the Itiwana were starting to feel less nervous about their leader's prolonged absence. While everyone would have preferred that their cunning kik-mongwi be present, Pahana was taking care of matters adequately. With the guidance of his mother and the rest of the Shakowin, he had managed to keep the tribe functioning well. He continued the training of the Two Horn Riders, mediated disputes, and oversaw the daily rituals. He carried himself in a very authoritative and chieftainly manner.

Pahana was usually accompanied everywhere by Calian, O'Yewa, and Masewa. However, during his duration as tribal leader, he sent them to take his place as the war chief of the Two Horn Riders. He was too occupied with being the kik-mongwi to personally oversee the daily warrior training, so he passed that responsibility on to his formidable family members.

However, Pahana wasn't alone while performing his daily duties. He kept Hayoka constantly by his side during this period. Pahana wanted Hayoka to see that the Itiwana were a noble people, so he allowed his new friend to observe everything he did. Also, he was very accustomed to having his entourage of fellow warriors constantly at his side to whom he could talk. He enjoyed knowing someone was listening to his ideas. Hayoka acted as a substitute.

Hayoka, who was quite clever and a very quick study, took in everything. He watched, and he listened and absorbed every single facet of Itiwana life. He was even permitted to attend meetings of the Shakowin. Most of the Shakowin members were not happy about this, causing a rift in the council. Pinga, however, sided with her offspring because Tawa had approved of Hayoka remaining among them. She also supported anything that would make her son's time as chieftain easier. She hoped having a friend at his side would ease the pressure on him, so she persuaded Atira, Manabazo, and T'Soona to tolerate Hayoka's presence at the proceedings.

Hayoka remained as unobtrusive and inconspicuous as he could, not wanting to do anything that would cause the Shakowin to be angry with him. He was a silent shadow on the wall, a mute witness to the deepest workings of the Itiwana.

The more I learn, the more I think these Itiwana are a good people, he mused. *But I must observe more before I make a determination.*

Atira carefully watched Hayoka during these meetings because her memories of his father's betrayal made her extremely wary of him. Hobomok had always desired her, which was a large part of the friction between him and Yana-Luha that resulted in his betrayal. *I trust him like a fly trusts a spider.*

And Atira was not the only one to suspiciously observe the northerner. No one was more disturbed about Pahana's growing bond with Hayoka than Calian. Having been sent to act as a surrogate war chief, he was unable to stay close to Pahana, and therefore he could not listen in on the conversations between the clan elder-son and Hayoka.

Calian didn't like that Hayoka was attached to Pahana's side like a tick. They were clearly forming a bond. The more they spent time together, the more they formed a connection. It was hard for Calian to watch for signs of trouble while he was separated from the man he was supposed to be watching.

Calian was especially upset when Pahana came to him and asked Calian to choose a bison mount for Hayoka to ride—something that was usually reserved only for a warrior of the Two Horn Riders.

"You're giving one of our bison to the visitor?" Calian asked, doing his best to remain respectful. "This is against your father's rule. Are you defying Tawa's authority?"

Pahana seemed annoyed by the implication. "I did not tell you my mind to be flayed for it. Even family members should know when they are being disrespectful to their leader."

"You always have my respect, noble clan elder-son."

"I had always thought so," Pahana said gruffly, and then his expression lightened up. "Ah, but what fools we are to raise voices at each other. You worry overmuch, Calian. Just do as I ask. I intend to make Hayoka an honorary member of the Itiwana and then begin his training as a member of the Two Horn Riders. I'm sure my father will approve once he gets to know Hayoka well. Be at ease, brave Calian. All will be well."

As Pahana walked away, Calian felt a tightness in his stomach. He was becoming more and more disturbed. *I swore to Tawa that I would keep watch on Hayoka, and I must find a way to do so.*

Young Kia had never been burdened with such a difficult decision to make. She desperately wanted to use her ever-increasing power to help the Itiwana of Shipapa-Lina, especially her parents. She was raised to worship the Sky Elders and to serve them. However, she had not been able to bring herself to disobey her mentor.

She continued to train in the use of her power but had avoided any further visualizing of the spirit world. She shied away from communicating with Shula-Witsa again because she did not want to tell one of the great Elders that she was refusing their request. The earth and the sky were fighting a war, and she hated the idea of being idle while gods and men died.

Sitting cross-legged in a kiva, she wondered what was happening to the brave Itiwana who did not avoid combat. What could her father be doing now? She hadn't seen him in almost a year. He was a ruler of a tribe at war. What challenges was he facing?

Kia chose to attempt the Dream Guessing Rite to find out whether her family was healthy and well. She covered her face with an eyeless, ceremonial cornhusk mask. Breathing deeply, she let her mind slip into a relaxed state, akin to the beginning of sleep. Once in this half-awake state, she stretched her unrestrained instincts out into the physical world. Entire plains and vistas of Ulah-Nane were within the scope of her unconstrained perceptions. She saw men and monsters, fish and fowl.

And then she saw Shipapa-Lina. Her unfettered spirit entered her home, unseen by anyone. She saw her mother, who seemed sad. She saw her brother, who was in the company of a stranger. But she did not see her father. Her senses flooded across the village, but there was no sign of Tawa. She detected a pensive feeling among the Itiwana. Everyone seemed very worried, due to their leader's absence.

Where are you, father? I must know.

The moon had risen and Pahana had retired for the night. Hayoka was given a pit house to sleep in during his stay. It sat upon the top of the mesa, above the cliff housing. Unable to sleep, he decided to take a walk around Shipapa-Lina. He had spent all his recent days in the company of Pahana and had barely had a moment alone to reflect.

Hayoka liked occasional solitude and he needed this time alone. No one was visible except a few sentries at the outskirts of the village. This suited Hayoka just fine. He did not like the suspicious stares he got from members of the Itiwana tribe.

Hayoka walked past the Speaking Mound, toward the village clearing, savoring the quiet and the coolness of the night. He looked up at the stars and thought that they seemed so different from the stars in the north. *Shipapa-Lina is a much nicer village than Teketsertok, but it is still not home.*

Hayoka noticed someone moving and turned to see Calian lurking in the shadows, watching him like a predator. Hayoka was surprised that Calian could sneak up on him, but this Calian seemed full of surprises.

"Hello, Calian," he said casually. "It's a fine moon."

"I suppose it is," Calian replied. "What are you doing skulking out here so late?"

"Simply walking, my friend," Hayoka said with a polite smile. "Nothing more. I like to walk at night."

"And I like to watch at night," Calian said. "You can never tell what you'll see. Don't you agree?"

Hayoka knew what Calian was really saying, and he was not afraid to match wits with the distrustful Itiwana. "Oh, I agree, I agree. I'm sorry there's nothing interesting for you to watch tonight. You must be so disappointed."

"On the contrary," Calian replied. "I'm patient. Persistence is a gift."

"I agree," Hayoka responded. "I'm patient, also. And I plan to be here for some time and take many walks."

"You should sleep more," Calian said. "It's healthier."

"I could say the same to you, good Calian."

Calian's eyes locked coldly with the other man's. "I think we understand each other."

"We do," Hayoka said. "It's nice to be understood. Ah well, I think I'll go to my bed now. Enjoy your night, son of Pogum."

"I am enjoying it, son of Hobomok."

"So am I."

Hayoka walked back up the mesa to the section of Shipapa-Lina where his pit house was. Calian kept watch on him until his view was obscured by an old longhouse. Hayoka had expected Calian to follow covertly, but the suspicious warrior did not. Hayoka suspected that the only reason Calian wasn't trailing him was because he knew Calian was there. Hayoka expected to have more such confrontations with Calian in the future.

After climbing down into the pit house, Hayoka heard someone—or something—moving in the dark, and this time it wasn't Calian. He spotted a silhouette via a dim light from outside. It wasn't very big, and it seemed to be either hunched over or walking on all fours. The ears seemed to stand upward, coming to a point. The mysterious figure was brightly colored. It seemed to have fur and perhaps even a fuzzy tail. The creature could have been a fox, but it was far too large. It was closer to the size of a large wolf.

Hayoka feared whatever this creature was and attempted to climb back up the ladder. The creature, however, suddenly popped into view, pulling Hayoka down from the ladder with a clawed paw. The moonlight beaming down illuminated the mystery being.

Hayoka gasped when he discovered the intruder was a very large, white snow fox. The oversized fox looked at Hayoka with coal-black, intelligent eyes. It sniffed him, and then it spoke.

"Worry not, Hayoka," the foxlike creature said. "A friend I am. Agwara, my name is. The snow fox spirit, I am. Come to warn you, I have. Beware, you must be of the Itiwana. Dangerous, they are. Your destruction they will cause. Wait to see. The Itiwana are evil. Hayoka must strike first. Destroy them, you must. Destroy the Itiwana."

CHAPTER TEN

T awa had seen two full moons come and go
since he left Shipapa-Lina, which meant
he had been away for more than a month. It got
colder every day as he moved farther from the
tree Yaxche and within the range of the winds
of Wuchowson. He cut some time off his trip by
using the stolen Vykan longship to sail north up
the Endless River Agazzi. Without extra men to
row, he used the longship's sail to catch the wind.
The Itiwana had had no conception of a sailing
ship or how sails worked before they encountered
the Vykans. It was an interesting invention.

Brave Fire lay calmly in the center of the boat,
looking curiously out at the water and coastline.
Occasionally, Tawa steered them to the shore and

allowed Brave Fire to eat and stretch its legs and graze. Tawa also had to find fresh water for himself and his mount. Then he would return to the boat, lead Brave Fire aboard, and resume his trip north up the Agazzi River.

He reached the point where the Endless River Agazzi connected to the Ice Wolf River and went farther north. He sailed through the cold realm of Norumbega, where the Vykans had once lived before relocating to Vineland. He had come here once before to battle the Wendigo.

Tawa prayed to Awona'Wilona that all the Vykans were gone. He was fairly sure they hadn't forgotten about the Itiwana killing Giwakna, or Tawa himself killing the Berserker. They did not strike him as the forgiving type.

He proceeded deeper into Norumbega, but he eventually lost the wind. Unable to row the longship alone, especially with a heavy bison aboard, he had to make for the shore. He did not want to be spotted by some enemy while floating blatantly like a duck on the water.

Once on the shore, he lowered his sail and used foliage to conceal the boat as efficiently as possible. He led Brave Fire to some grass and allowed the beast to graze again. The big bison was so well trained, it didn't stray too far from its master. He sat and ate an apple, waiting for the wind to return so he could continue his voyage.

Soon, Tawa felt the wind begin to kick up. It was a relief at first, as he went to collect Brave Fire, but then he became concerned as the wind suddenly became very powerful. It started to howl as if a storm was coming. The strangest part was that the sky and clouds had not changed at all.

This is beginning to look familiar, he thought.

He saw what appeared to be another mini cyclone. It brought to his mind the day Dagwona attacked Shipapa-Lina. The twister moved closer, and the winds whipped to hurricane levels. Tawa had to grab hold of a tree to root himself; otherwise, the wind would toss him around like a leaf. Even the bulky Brave Fire was feeling threatened by the power of the wind.

It's that cursed Dagwona again! He thought.

The wind stopped as suddenly as it started. The small cyclone vanished, only to be replaced by a familiar woman. Tawa let go of the tree and rushed to Brave Fire, pulling Dragonfly from the bison's harness. He recognized his attacker. The woman glared hatefully at him.

"Dagwona," Tawa said. "Again, we play this lethal game. I don't suppose you're ready to switch to the Blessing Way, are you?"

"Stupid statement."

"I thought as much," Tawa said warily. He wondered what he was in for. He tightened his grip on the Dragonfly. As she took a step closer, he raised his weapon. "I'm ready for you. Come ahead, Witch!"

"She shall," Dagwona said. "Perish painfully!"

Dagwona raised her hands, and a funnel of hurricane-level winds assaulted Tawa, causing him to stagger backward. He braced himself after back peddling for a few yards. Tawa was a mastop-kachina and had a rare vigor that made him highly resilient. Despite the howling, unyielding wind, he pushed himself forward, inching toward his foe, spear in hand.

"No nearer!" Dagwona shouted in fury. "Fall, fool!"

The witch increased the airstream, which halted Tawa's forward progress. When the gusts began to push him back once more, Tawa jabbed the Dragonfly into the ground. He knew that once Dragonfly was embedded into a solid object, it could not be removed by anyone except Tawa himself—not even a witch.

With all the power of a mastop-kachina, Tawa grasped the spear with desperate strength and an unshakable will. Barely able to maintain his grip, Tawa utilized a technique that Manabazo had taught him years ago. Tawa used the properties of the magic spear to draw natural power from the land. His blood contained the blood of the kachina earth spirits, which he could replenish from the soil. Renewed strength flooded into him. Energized by the primal energies of Ulah-Nane, Tawa was revitalized.

I will not be pushed back! Tawa thought, fighting off fear as well as wind.

Dagwona's face registered her shock at seeing this Itiwana resist the awesome force of her cyclone. "It's impossible," she squealed.

She intensified the windstorm so forcefully, Tawa's feet were blown out from under him. With a rigid, unyielding grip, Tawa urgently clutched onto the Dragonfly for his very life. He was like a leaf fluttering on a tree branch, suspended in the tumultuous airflow. His fingers gripped the spear as tightly as a constricting serpent would squeeze its prey. *I will never let go!*

Tawa hoped the witch would burn herself out and exhaust her power before Tawa's grip slackened. It was a test of will as well as power.

Where are you, father? Kia wondered.

Kia had spent an entire day searching Ulah-Nane with all her arcane senses. She was becoming quite nervous about being unable to locate her father. Clearly, he was much farther from Shipapa-Lina than she had anticipated. She had never been outside the Land of Everlasting Summer herself. Her experience had been limited to Shipapa-Lina and Kolhu. Kia was amazed by the astounding things she was seeing as her unleashed senses expanded across the vast land.

She used the ceremonial azure flame of the kiva, despite not wanting to connect with Shula-Witsa. She worried that the Elder would contact her through the elemental flame, and she did not want to oppose or provoke a mighty Sky Elder at a time like this. Kia did not want to be distracted from her task. *Where is my father?*

She had to stop and rest several times because this exertion was so fatiguing. She fell asleep several times between efforts. She would then awaken and chastise herself for taking too much time resting. Then she would rush back to the flame to scan the world for her missing father.

She was losing hope of finding him when she finally sensed his familiar aura. Focusing her fantastic powers, she discovered him far up north. Kia gasped in panic when she saw that he was in deadly danger.

"Father! Oh no!" she cried in alarm.

Kia stared, horrified, watching the image of her father hanging onto Dragonfly as devastating winds battered him. She saw the Witch of the Whirlwind trying mercilessly to slay Kia's beloved father.

"What do I do?" Kia gasped fearfully.

Abruptly, a red eye appeared and gazed hauntingly at her. "Oh!" she cried, startled.

"Help your father," Shula-Witsa said urgently. "Help him!"

"I want to," Kia answered, almost in tears. "But Molowia..."

"Defy her wishes!" the Elder said. "Defy her!"

Kia fervently wanted to disobey Molowia's command to remain neutral in the war, but still hesitated to defy her teacher. The young girl sat torn between her love for her father and her devotion to Molowia.

"Tawa will die!" Shula-Witsa roared. "He will."

"No!" Kia shouted. "He mustn't die! Not my father!"

"Then save him!" the Elder ordered. "Save him!"

Shula-Witsa's fiery eye shined its flickering, hypnotic light into the girl's youthful eyes. Kia stared fixedly into that eerie light as his words echoed in her distraught brain. She found herself unable to think of anything else other than rescuing her imperiled father.

"Yes, I must!" Kia yelled. "I must save him, no matter what the cost!"

CHAPTER ELEVEN

Must ... hang ... on! Tawa thought.

Tawa's grip was beginning to weaken as the stormy winds battered him relentlessly. Despite the power he had absorbed from Ulah-Nane, his muscles had their limits. He knew he only had moments left before his fingers lost their strength.

However, he thought he felt the winds weakening. His feet were no longer suspended in the air. Surely, even the witch had her limits. Was Dagwona nearing hers? *Is she weakening? I need only keep hold a bit longer. If I can outlast her attack...*

Before he got the opportunity to discover whether or not he could win a battle of endurance, he saw Dagwona turn her focus to the Endless River Agazzi. He craned his neck to see a section of the river begin to bubble. A geyser of blue water spit upward.

What's happening now? Tawa wondered.

With an angry growl, Wishpoosh rose from the water. The massive beaver spirit, with a stony, spiked tail, waded to the shore, eyes fixed savagely upon Dagwona. It reeked of power.

When Dagwona saw Wishpoosh approaching, she cried out in alarm. No wind could move this monstrous guardian of the Itiwana. She had never expected to see this powerful creature so far from Kolhu. It ignored the hurricane gusts as it marched onto the land. Despite her formidable abilities, she knew when she was outmatched.

Distracted and afraid, she lost concentration, and the winds stopped blowing. She backed away, clearly intimidated. Dagwona upstretched her arms, causing an updraft of wind that levitated her above the ground.

Free of the wind squall, the exhausted Itiwana leader took a moment to wiggle his cramped fingers, then pulled Dragonfly from the ground and marched toward the Witch of the Whirlwind.

"No spirit for battling Wishpoosh?" Tawa replied. "Where are you going, Witch?"

"Seeking someone's son," Dagwona. "Killing kin. Punish Pahana."

Tawa angrily screamed, "You will not touch my son!"

Tawa quickly raised his spear and aimed it at the Whirlwind Witch. At the same time, she summoned a wind to help her escape. Tawa threw his spear, but it was too late. Dagwona used a gust of wind force to lift her in the air, and the spear missed.

The winds carried her to the sky, and she cried out, "Feel fear. We will win."

Tawa could only watch her float away. He gritted his teeth and cursed the Whirlwind Witch. He feared for his Son. *Cursed witch. I pray she stays far from my boy and the rest of my family. She won't kill Pahana herself while he's in Shipapa-Lina with Manabazo, but will she send someone else to do it? And if she does, I pray that the boy is equal to the task of defending himself and the tribe. I hope Manabazo can advise them.*

Tawa turned his attention to Wishpoosh. "Once again, I thank you, mighty Wishpoosh."

Wishpoosh did not respond. It sank back into the river and vanished. Tawa wondered how the creature happened to be here. He assumed it must be Molowia who sent it, as she did when the Vykans attacked Shipapa-Lina.

"Are you watching me, Molowia?" he said loudly. "Once more, I am in your debt."

Moments later, a swirling cloud of mist appeared. Tawa wasn't frightened, assuming it was Molowia contacting him. The strange, misty substance slowly materialized in front of him. Tawa expected to see his shaman aunt. The kik-mongwi's eyebrows raised in surprise when he saw the ghostly cloud form into the image of his own daughter.

"Hello, father," the phantom image of the girl said.

"Kia?" Tawa said. "Was it you who sent Wishpoosh to my aid?"

"I did, father," she said. "I could not bear to see you harmed."

Tawa managed a smile. "I would not like to see that myself. Thank you, sweet daughter. I must admit, I am impressed that you had the power to control Wishpoosh at so young an age."

Kia was glad to hear that she had impressed her father. "I don't control Wishpoosh. No one truly controls him. We have an understanding. I was able to convince him."

"The intervention was timely," Tawa said. "I wish I could count on his help during the rest of my journey."

"I wish I could do that for you, father," she said regretfully. "But Molowia will not allow it. Wishpoosh must protect Kolhu."

"I understand," Tawa said. "And what of you, my dearest daughter? Can I count on you for help?"

Kia's face announced her sadness. "I don't know, father. Molowia will not be pleased. When she realizes what I've done, she may forbid me from helping you again. I'm sorry."

"I understand," he told her softly. "It's not your fault. I am very glad for the help you supplied, and I'm very proud of what you've done. Look at you.

You've grown so. I wish I could lift you in my arms and embrace you as I did when you were little."

"Must you continue into danger?"

"You know the answer to that, little one," Tawa said. "Our family has a duty. I do what I must do for the good of the Itiwana. I must continue on my way. But I ask you to use your amazing powers to look after your older brother. The Witch of the Whirlwind has threatened him, and it would be a relief to my troubled brow if I knew your power was guarding his back."

"I promise I will, father," she said. "Pahana will be kept safe."

"You're a good girl, Kia," he said. "You do our family proud. It was wonderful to see your precious face again. And remember, I love you dearly."

The image of Kia displayed the tears her true body shed. "I love you very much, father. Please be careful. Goodbye."

The vision of Kia disappeared. Tawa took a moment to think about his family, especially concerned about his son. He forced himself to focus on his task. Tawa needed to continue his journey. He hoped to battle Nanook and get back to Shipapa-Lina as quickly as he could.

Speed was doubly important now. He not only needed to return home before the cold weather came in earnest, but his children also needed him. As a father, he wished he could head home immediately to defend them, but knew that was not an option. *I must be a chieftain before a father.*

He noted that some heavy winds remained after Dagwona's departure. That would make sailing easier. He swiftly retrieved his bison mount, leading the animal back to the longship, which he shoved into the river. Coxing his mount onboard, he raised the sail again. He hoped Dagwona was so intimidated by her encounter with Wishpoosh, she wouldn't be back. *It's a slim hope, but I can wish.*

They kept moving farther north until they reached Gitche Gumee, which was the most massive lake in the northern part of Ulah-Nane. It was once the lair of the Wendigo, Giwakna. The remains of the Vykan encampment could be seen there. After another break, Tawa set sail once again and began his attempt to cross the Gitche Gumee in winter.

The winter months were coming, and without the stable weather provided by Yaxche, Tawa was beginning to feel the cold. He had prepared for this and brought a wolf's pelt to wrap around his shoulders. He also had an extra-long deerskin breechcloth around his waist and additional fur lining inside his moccasins. The threatening cold was becoming increasingly uncomfortable, but he would not let that stop him from performing his debt of honor.

"Disloyal!" Molowia shouted angrily. "Unacceptable! You have betrayed me! Betrayed Kolhu! I never would have expected this of you."

Kia stood before Molowia in the Sun Dagger house, nervous about facing her mentor's anger. "I didn't betray anyone, Cacique. I merely helped my father. What's wrong with that?"

Molowia narrowed her eyes, exasperated. She gritted her teeth. "You made a vow to obey me if I agreed to teach you. Your father and I agreed on this."

"But..."

"Silence and listen!" Molowia yelled. "We here at Kolhu were meant to be neutral in this war, including you. You may have impulsively brought the evil of the Enemy Way down upon us. And by sending Wishpoosh away, you left Kolhu vulnerable had anyone attacked us at that moment. You were selfish and irresponsible, and you did all this without consulting me. I rule here. You should have asked me before taking such drastic actions, especially in defiance of my edict. You defied me. That's as bad as lying to me. It's a betrayal of trust!"

"I am sorry for disobeying you," Kia said. "But my father needed me. I had to do it."

"You act as a child, not a future leader," Molowia said, distressed and angry. "Clearly, you are not yet old enough to make the kind of decisions that come with power like ours. I believe your training should be halted."

"What?" Kia cried. "But why? That's unfair."

Molowia held up her hand for silence. "Speak no more. You need to mature before you can be trusted with the abilities I wish to teach you. You are already too powerful for one so young."

"Cacique, please, I..."

"Silence!" Molowia ordered. "You need to become an adult before you can become a shaman. I will teach you no more until you act as an adult."

Molowia stomped out of the chamber, leaving a devastated Kia alone. *This is not fair! She can't do this to me. How can she punish me like this for helping my father? It's so wrong!*

Kia knew she would have to learn more shamanic magic and increase her power if she was going to help Shipapa-Lina and keep her promise to protect her brother. She had to continue her training. But she needed a new teacher.

The heartbroken Kia felt she had only one choice. Lighting a new fire in the kiva pit, she focused her mind on contacting the one being who she knew would teach her the things she needed to learn if she was to battle the Enemy Way.

That strange but familiar eye appeared in the fire once again. The intimidating voice of Shula-Witsa spoke to her once more. "You called me? You called?"

"Yes," Kia replied. "I need your help. I need you to teach me. I will serve the Sky Elders however you wish. I am no longer neutral. I will be your weapon of war."

"That is good," Shula-Witsa said. "Very good."

"Will you teach me?" she asked.

"I'll teach you," the fire Elder said. "I will. You'll learn much. You will. We'll fight together. We will."

"Yes," Kia said. "We will. Together."

It had been well over a month since Tawa left Shipapa-Lina in Pahana's care. Despite the tense feeling in the air, Pahana had been enjoying his time as the kik-mongwi. He was also enjoying the company of his new friend, Hayoka. They had become close during the past month. Pahana was determined to make Hayoka into one of his Two Horn Riders. He had been giving riding lessons to the northerner. Hayoka's bison was named Gray Shadow. Hayoka chose that name due to the way most of the Itiwana felt about him. They looked at him like he was a shadow on the honor of the Itiwana.

Pahana did not seem to care what the rest of the tribe was saying about the visitor. Regardless of their doubts and despite the objections of Atira and Calian, the resolute Pahana got his way, with the backing of Pinga.

Pahana had set his mind on showing Hayoka all the best aspects of the Itiwana. That meant anointing him the honor of being one of the Two Horn Riders. He hoped that the camaraderie of the noble warriors would be the best way of reversing Hayoka's negative opinion of his family. He also wanted to show the Itiwana he had the wit to turn a possible enemy into a friend. Aside from all that, he simply liked Hayoka.

When he had free time, Pahana oversaw Hayoka's training on his new mount. Hayoka was initially resistant, never having ridden any type of mount before. He knew deep down that he had never been a natural warrior. He was more of a planner or sneak attack specialist. He preferred to wait until conditions were to his advantage before he attacked anyone. Pahana was now trying to force Hayoka to change to a fighting style he was uncomfortable with. As much as he tried, he couldn't talk Pahana out of this unshakable notion of turning Hayoka into a great Two Horn Rider.

Hayoka kept thinking about his encounter with Agwara the Snow Fox Spirit. The strange being had shown up to warn him that the Itiwana would eventually destroy him unless he destroyed them first. He had not told anyone about Agwara's visit because he still wasn't entirely sure who he could trust among the Itiwana. Would they believe him? Would they accuse him of being in league with Agwara? He did not want to take the chance.

He continued biding his time, attempting to determine who among them was his friend and who was his enemy. He knew Calian was his enemy, but who else was a threat? Could they all be dangerous to him, as Agwara had suggested? It seemed hard to believe, but Hayoka did not dismiss the possibility.

Since Pahana was too busy acting as chieftain of the tribe, he turned Hayoka's training over to O'Yewa and Masewa. Their job, after all, was to train potential Two Horn Riders. They did as their cousin commanded and took Hayoka under their combined wings.

Calian was also involved in training the mounted warriors but refused to have any part in teaching Hayoka. Pahana knew of Calian's disdain for Hayoka and ordered the twin brothers to keep Calian away from Hayoka. Calian, however, was watching—always watching, just as Tawa had requested.

Whatever he may be up to, he'll find me ready to stop him, Calian thought.

Calian didn't know that Hayoka had a formidable ally. Close by, Agwara the Snow Fox Spirit was secretly observing the tribe. He sneakily came near, especially at night, making note of the warrior's training. The fox was particularly interested in Hayoka's progress. Agwara avoided Manabazo, fearing that the Elder would sense his presence.

Agwara was not always alone. Sometimes, Dagwona, the Whirlwind Witch, also lurked in the foliage, watching the Itiwana. She could not attack the village directly because of Manabazo's presence. Also, she knew Pahana and Pinga had the power to drive her away. But despite being unable to destroy them in a direct attack, she still intended to keep her vow to kill Tawa's son.

"Fools the Itiwana are," Agwara said to her. "Realize they do not that they have a viper growing in their midst. Destruction from within, eventually will we see."

"Whirlwind Witch won't wait," Dagwona said. "She shall soon see son slain. Eldest eradicated earliest. Punish Pahana. Terminate tomorrow."

"As you wish. Tomorrow, does Pahana die."

CHAPTER TWELVE

O n a damp morning, Pahana woke early and decided it was time he gave Hayoka some personal attention. He had been allowing others to handle Hayoka's training for weeks, but now felt it was time to see for himself how the newcomer was progressing.

Oblivious to the fact that Dagwona and Agwara had targeted him for death, he walked to the pit house before dawn and roughly woke Hayoka up for some riding practice. "Up, lazy fellow. No one becomes great by sleeping all day."

Hayoka was rather disgruntled about being unexpectedly roused before the cock crowed. Regardless, he reluctantly complied with the clan elder-son's wishes and followed Pahana into the humid air.

"What are we doing today?" Hayoka asked.

"Learning," Pahana said.

Pahana woke his grandmother to tell her he was leaving Shipapa-Lina for a short trip. She was angry about this, scolding him for leaving the village while Tawa was away. "Have you learned nothing from your last inexcusable absence?"

"Calm down, grandmother," he said. "It's just a quick jaunt. I'll be back before the midday meal is served. I leave you in charge while I'm gone."

"Your devotion to this new friend you've made is inexplicable," she said. "But I see your mind is made up. I won't fight you on this, but if something happens while you are absent..."

"No need for worry," Pahana said. "I'll be back in the blink of an eye."

Though she had the power to overrule him, she chose to let him have his way. As she watched him stride haughtily away, concerned about the influence Hayoka was having on him, she sent someone to deliver a message to Calian. *The boy is disappointing me.*

Pahana led the sleepy Hayoka to the bison pens, and the wolf Chybiabis followed behind his master dutifully. The young pen attendants quickly got World Giant and Gray Shadow ready to be taken out for a ride.

Minutes later, just as Hayoka was hopping up on his mount, Calian came running to catch up with them. Pahana was surprised to see him, while Hayoka was annoyed by the sight of him.

"Ho, good Pahana," Calian said.

"Calian? Going fishing, are you?" Pahana asked. "You're awake early."

"I could not sleep," Calian answered. "I spotted you walking here, and I came to join you."

Hayoka sneered. "How splendid for us."

Pahana did not completely believe Calian had just happened to see them walking but did not want to call his friend and kin a liar. "Wonderful as your company always is, this journey is for we two alone. I would take this trek with Hayoka only. I am decided. We will not stay for our morning meal."

"Your word stands unquestioned," Calian said. "I would not ever think of disobeying."

"Good."

"Yet, I would request to accompany you," Calian continued. "Would you refuse an uncle and fellow warrior who has been like a brother to you through dangers untold and enemies uncounted?"

Pahana was moved by the plea from his beloved kinsman. "I'll compromise with you. Finish the morning training session with the Two Horn Riders and then follow our tracks. Consider it a test. If you can track us, you can join us."

Calian was not happy with the proposed compromise, but it was the best agreement he was likely to get. Pahana was not a man to change his mind easily, especially when influenced by this Hayoka scoundrel.

"A wise and fair decision, Kik-Mongwi," Calian said. "It will be as you say."

"Let it be so," Pahana said. "I ride now. I shall expect you before the day gets hot. And you, Hayoka... come. We ride."

As Pahana cantered off upon World Giant, Hayoka nudged Gray Shadow to follow. Calian made eye contact with Hayoka, and the two glared contemptuously at each other. Hayoka was relieved that Calian was not coming along, but was also disappointed to hear that he would be joining them later.

He'll be trouble for me, without doubt, Hayoka thought.

Calian watched with anxious concern as the two men trotted out of the village, with Chybiabis running behind them.

Someone else watched Pahana and Hayoka leave Shipapa-Lina. Concealed in some distant trees, Dagwona and Agwara were still observing. The plotting pair were happy to see Pahana riding away from his tribe with only a single companion.

"Excellent event," Dagwona said with a satisfied grin. "Two trek toward trouble. Pathetic Pahana perishes. Death draws due."

"Fortunate this is," the snow fox spirit said. "Into our hands, the young fool walks. Easier this will be. No help will he have this day. Die he will, as a message to Tawa."

Molowia couldn't sleep. Her angst was partly due to her psychic instincts buzzing relentlessly in her head. She was overwhelmed by a primal sensation of coming danger. This was not new, but it was worse on this particular night. The other reason she found sleep evasive was the problem with Kia. She felt bad about having to punish the girl, but she was also angry about the betrayal of trust.

She didn't relish the idea of slowing Kia's training at a time when unpredictable peril was gathering everywhere. Kolhu could come under attack at any time. Even with Wishpoosh protecting the city, the leader of this community needed to have the power to defend it. If anything unfortunate should happen to Molowia, Kia would be tasked with protecting Kolhu.

Molowia was doubting her decision, but she chose to stand firm. She and Wishpoosh would have to defend Kolhu alone, at least until Kia grew up. If the war lasted another ten years, Kia would have ample time to become an adult and make better decisions.

I wonder what she's doing now, Molowia mused.

Kia felt the exaltation of power. Directing her mystic energy to the sipapu in the floor of the Sun Dagger house, she had conjured up a dimensional portal to the spirit realm. *I've done it!*

As Kia gazed into the portal, she saw through the veil of reality, peering into another realm. To her amazement, she was seeing things few mortals had ever witnessed. Just as she had explored Ulah-Nane with her expanded senses, she surveyed this new, alien plain.

Her efforts to pierce the walls of earthly reality became easier by the hour. At one point in her search, frightening tentacles emerged from the sipapu portal. Alarmingly, they stretched out and tried to grab her. After a moment of panic, she was able to defend herself with her shamanic power. She hurled fireballs at the snakelike appendages, driving them back into the portal. The whole experience would have terrified her weeks ago.

But now she loved it. Hour by hour, she was gaining more control over forces that even the most experienced shaman feared to trifle with. Kia, however, was confident that she was not simply a mortal. She was a mastop-kachina-demi-Elder-shaman. Kia was the first of her kind.

I can master this! I can master anything! I will become the bane of the Enemy Way.

All the while, the unblinking eye of Shula-Witsa stared at her from out of the portal. It locked its gaze on her, burning unremittingly into her brain and mesmerizing her. The Sky Elder manipulated the girl, intending to turn her into his fist of war.

Tawa had finally reached Vineland in the cold northern regions. He had never been this far from home before, and he had never experienced such cold temperatures. He was worried about his son and wondered what was happening back in Shipapa-Lina. At the moment, he had a more imminent problem.

As he climbed out of his longship with his bison, his heart beat with trepidation. He had reached his goal. Now, he would have to battle a powerful and deadly poshayanki. *It's time.*

He had feared the poshayanki ever since his encounter with the horrible A'Chiyala when he was young. Now he had to fight one alone. He took Dragonfly from the harness and gripped the spear tightly, knowing it was his only hope of survival. The only other weapon he had was a small pouch of powder Manabazo had instructed T'Soona to concoct for him.

He rode his mount from the shore, taking deep breaths to calm himself before the combat. After a short trip, Tawa found the cave Pinga had directed him to. Tawa saw the huge bear paw prints on the snowy ground, and his fear increased.

Nanook must be very big, he thought. Saying a quick prayer, he entered the cavern with great apprehension.

Tawa crept into the cave, his heart pounding and all his senses on high alert. He was facing his greatest fear... a poshayanki. As he moved farther into the cave, the dimming light made him more pensive. As the shadows increased, he could not help imaging what was hiding in them. Tawa felt his hands tremble slightly as he anticipated something jumping out at him.

A fearsome roar announced his opponent's arrival. Out from the darkened rear section of the cave came the biggest bear Tawa had ever seen. The albino beast walked on its hind legs. At 15 feet, its head almost touched the roof of the cave. Its 2,000-plus pound frame lumbered toward the Itiwana. Sharp claws and teeth glinted in the dim light of the cave. The creature's roar echoed in the cave and made Tawa want to cover his ears. The beast's eyes seemed to glow yellow as it charged at the intruder with savage, murderous intent. Tawa fought the urge to flee and faced his fear.

Tawa drew back his arm to throw his spear, hoping to end this confrontation quickly. Nanook roared a more deafening, terrifying roar than before. It reverberated like a shock wave through the cavern. The burst of sound caused Tawa to shudder while tossing his weapon. The spear passed by Nanook harmlessly, embedding itself in the cave wall.

The big bear was not unintelligent, and it tried to grab the spear out of the wall. Nanook cupped his enormous paws around the projectile weapon. However, even the giant bear could not remove the enchanted Dragonfly from the wall.

Tawa leaped forward, needing the weapon desperately. His only option was to toss that powder which he had brought in preparation for this contest. He pulled it out of the pouch of powder and threw it at Nanook. The potion exploded into a gray mist that blinded the big bear. Nanook coughed as he breathed in the smoke. Blinded, it clawed at the air savagely.

Tawa leaped, flipped, and rebounded onto his feet, reaching the spear and pulling it from the cave wall. The blinded bear lashed out for Tawa, but the Itiwana jabbed at it with his spear. Lunging forward, Nanook tried to pin Tawa to the ground, hoping to rip his throat out. However, Tawa fended off the beast's fangs with his spear. Employing his warrior skills, he used the creature's own bestial recklessness against it, leading the beast to the narrower cave mouth, where the beast hit its head on the roof of the cave. The distraction allowed Tawa to stab the creature in the foot.

Wounded and limping, Nanook continued to attack with no plan... only fury. The creature continued to slash at Tawa but couldn't connect with the agile Itiwana, who chopped at those lethal paws with the spear. Tawa kept jabbing the big bear with Dragonfly, wearing away at the monster. Tawa was smarter and more skillful in combat than anyone the bestial poshayanki had encountered before, and Dragonfly was the ultimate monster-killing weapon.

The fifteen-foot-tall beast stumbled around, its vision still impaired. It swung its big arm wildly and connected by sheer luck. It tore a painful wound in the chieftain. Nanook knocked the bloodied Tawa to the ground.

Despite the pain of being slashed open, Tawa rolled with the impact and quickly bounced back to his feet. The beast's sight was returning, and it used its keen nose to hone in on Tawa, chasing him around the cave. Tawa used a hit-and-run style, stabbing frantically at his pursuer. Eventually, the multiple spear wounds began to weaken the huge poshayanki.

Even a poshayanki can bleed, Tawa thought, seeing the open wounds on the bear.

This realization brought him new confidence, despite his own wound. The Itiwana chieftain continued to bounce around the cave, finally choosing to lure the beast outside, where there was more space to fight. As Tawa had hoped, Nanook got mad enough to follow him.

Tawa backed out of the cave into the open air. With more room to maneuver, he began to believe he still had a chance to survive this. The enraged Nanook lumbered out of the cave. They stood face-to-face out in the snow, pausing in their deadly combat as if in silent acknowledgment of respect for a worthy opponent. Their breath was visible in the air as they stood paused in their brief faceoff.

And then the beast roared and charged its prey, eager for the kill. Tawa raised the Dragonfly and ran toward his massive enemy. *This is it. This is my last chance. It ends now.*

The two foes closed for the final assault.

CHAPTER THIRTEEN

T awa and the terrifying Nanook charged recklessly toward each other in a final attempt
to destroy their opponent. The mastop-kachina
chieftain, armed only with the Dragonfly, ran
directly at the towering, savage beast. Tawa
ignored the pain and the bleeding. He knew
that he only had one chance to end this now, or
Nanook would surely end it first.

Tawa unexpectedly got some aid from an ally
he'd overlooked. Brave Fire, well-trained to pro-
tect its master, rammed its horns into Nanook.
Since these bison had been bred by the White
Buffalo Woman to be enemies of the poshayanki,
Brave Fire was able to wound the big bear in the leg.

Nanook let out of loud howl of agony. Tawa was elated by the assistance. He felt rather foolish for not thinking about using Brave Fire before now. He remembered the effect the bison had on A'Chiyala when the Itiwana had first found them. That was part of the reason his father, Yana-Luha, had chosen to use the bison as mounts, as well as food and plow animals.

How did I forget that? he chastised himself. *You're a fool, Tawa.*

Nanook, wounded in the left leg and the right foot, and its vision still blurred, turned its primal anger on the bison. It roared a challenge at the bison, telling it to retreat or fight. Brave Fire, prepared to charge. Head down, shoulders bunched, neck curved toward the bear, pawing the dirt, it snorted a reply to the challenge.

Tawa had one chance. While Nanook was focused on the bison, Tawa threw Dragonfly at the albino beast. His aim was true, and Dragonfly pierced Nanook's heart. Dragonfly piercing through Nanook's back, the point burst out of its chest.

The loudest cry of pain Tawa had ever heard erupted from the bear's throat. Blood spit from its mouth, and it looked up to the sky pleadingly, as if it were expecting help from its Winter Sky Elder masters. But no aid came.

With a sad, soft whimper, mighty Nanook fell to the snow. As its blood turned the snow red, Nanook whined a pathetic cry of defeat and pain.

Tawa came closer, yanking his spear out of the bear, causing it to cry out once again.

Barely alive, Nanook looked up pathetically at its killer. Tawa didn't know why he felt so bad about killing a poshayanki. They were agents of the Enemy Way, and they had to be destroyed. So why did he feel so vile?

As the dying Nanook gazed weakly up at him, Tawa felt such compassion for the bear that he kneeled down next to the dying beast. The poshayanki moved its mouth, and, to Tawa's surprise, it spoke.

"A ... fraid," Nanook said.

Tawa felt guilt and began to pet the bear gently. "Don't be afraid. Everything will be fine. Just close your eyes and rest."

Nanook closed its eyes and breathed its final breath. Tawa couldn't rid himself of the feeling of sadness at having killed Nanook. "I'm sorry," he whispered.

Tawa rose and took a moment to say a prayer for his enemy. He then patted Brave Fire on the neck. "Good boy. Thank you. You're a worthy successor to Mountain Fury."

He examined his gaping wound. He was losing blood from the gash in his abdomen where Nanook's all-too-sharp claws had slashed him. *This is looking bad*, he thought.

He removed the wolf's pelt from his shoulders and tied it tightly around his body, trying to stem the blood flow, as T'Soona had taught him to do.

He tried to stay calm, knowing that panic would make things worse.

The arrowhead, he thought. *That's why I'm here.*

He returned slowly to the cave, searching for the object he'd traveled so far to find. After stumbling around in the dark cave for what seemed to be an interminably long period of time, he spotted a soft, golden glow.

Lying on top of a pile of stone was a shining gold arrowhead. When he touched it, he felt that familiar sensation of divine energy that he'd felt when he touched the Tree of Life.

"The golden arrow of Awona'Wilona," he said. "This has not been in vain."

Tawa exited the cave, trying to ignore the pain of his wound and the frigid chill of the air. He slowly pulled himself up onto Brave Fire and nudged the loyal bison forward. He looked back at the large corpse of Nanook. He was feeling too weak to bury so large a creature, so he chose to leave Nanook as food for other animals.

As he began his long trip home with his prize, he worried about his ability to successfully make the trek. The pelt had only slowed the blood loss, not stopped it. Also, without the pelt wrapped around himself, his skin was exposed to the bitter cold. He wondered if he could endure the two physical threats to his life for the entire arduous journey back to his beloved Shipapa-Lina.

Pahana and Hayoka were heading back to Shipapa-Lina after romping through the woods for several hours. Chybiabis followed along with them. Pahana had given Hayoka a half day of riding lessons and was happy with the results he was seeing. True, Hayoka was still graceless and had a long way to go, but he was smart and learning fast.

I'll make a Two Horn Rider of him yet, Pahana thought.

The two young men were conversing and joking when Pahana spotted some familiar tracks on the ground. The son of Tawa seemed almost gleeful about spotting them. He pointed enthusiastically, crying out, "Look. Do you see them? Do you know what that means?"

Hayoka was a bit confused. "I'm afraid I don't..."

"It's Lucifee!" Pahana cried. "The cursed wildcat has foolishly wandered back to the Land of Everlasting Summer—a mistake. It escaped us previously, but by Awona'Wilona's blessed blood, I will have the beast now. You and I will strike like emissaries of death and bring the fanged fiend back to Shipapa-Lina so its hideous hide can adorn the Great Lodge. Come, we ride."

Hayoka remembered Lucifee well from their encounter. He recalled that the beast did not attack him, which had originated Calian's suspicions about him. He also remembered that the creature had called him "Coyote," a word that had been ringing in Hayoka's head ever since that day. Why had the Wildcat called him that, and why did it seem so familiar? Hayoka did not want Lucifee killed until he could ask the creature these questions. Also, the little voice which had always been whispering inside his head was insisting that he must not fight Lucifee.

Pahana began cantering forward, but noticed that his companion was not following. "Why the hesitation, Hayoka? I'm hungry for the kill. Never delay me when I'm hungry for a kill."

Hayoka had to do some fast thinking in order to contact Lucifee in case Pahana was able to succeed in his mission to kill the beast. "If you would indulge me, Kik-Mongwi, I would like to try catching the beast on my own. If it's agreeable to you, I suggest we separate. You've taught me so much today, and I am anxious to put your teachings into practice. Might I, I implore?"

Pahana laughed. "I admire your spirit, my friend, though not your humility. I swear, you amuse me. You're not ready to face the likes of Lucifee alone. Even if you were, I'm sure to get to him first. I have a personal grudge against that toothy villain. I won't let anyone deprive me of seeing him skinned alive, not even you, my eager friend. Still, if you wish to practice your hunting and riding skills while I do the difficult and deadly part, then be off with you. I'll wager you'll come back with nothing but an afternoon of exercise."

"I will endeavor to make myself worthy, good Pahana."

"Go earn respect, friend."

Pahana rode off with Chybiabis following behind him. Pahana was utterly determined to bring back Lucifee, although not necessarily in one piece. He had no plan, but possessed extraordinary confidence.

Hayoka paused, wondering how he could find Lucifee before Pahana got to him. Pahana was a great hunter, and he knew the region better. What chance did Hayoka have of beating him to the prize?

Hayoka's concentration was interrupted by a sudden strong wind. Initially, he gave it no weight. Then, however, he saw Dagwona, the Whirlwind Witch, descending from the sky. Hayoka stared in astonishment. *By all the Elders. This is the strangest thing I've yet seen.*

Dagwona touched down and smiled at Hayoka. "Glorious greetings. Whirlwind Witch wishes words with wandering warrior."

Kia was becoming more powerful than anyone would have dreamed possible. She obsessively practiced her new abilities every waking hour. Even while she ate, she mentally repeated the incantations she'd learned from Shula-Witsa.

Due to her relentless efforts, she was becoming a more forcible and effective shaman than Molowia could have predicted. Feeling a completeness that filled her soul, she was advancing beyond what any shaman in this world had ever been. Kia was becoming something new, something great, something remarkable and indescribable.

Shula-Witsa watched her with keen satisfaction. He knew he was recreating Kia, altering her into something that had never been seen in the mortal world before. The fiery Elder was quite satisfied with the weapon he was building. This child was surging with sheer power. The petite youngster was now something beyond human. She was growing into something that the Enemy Way would fear. This child would be the bane of the Enemy Way.

If she developed the way Shula-Witsa hoped, she would ultimately frighten any mortal or beast. When he was done with her, he would unleash her upon the servants of the Winter Elders. She would be a predator of skinwalkers and monsters. Shula-Witsa would turn Kia into the most magnificently terrifying weapon of destruction anyone had ever seen.

She was improving so quickly, Shula-Witsa had to speed up his training. Kia was already the first mastop-kachina-demi-Elder-shaman, and now was the first human to receive this level of training.

Kia herself was utterly fascinated and obsessed with learning more. She never stopped to think about what she was becoming. She never allowed herself to consider that she was transforming into something unknown. She merely continued practicing, savoring her escalating abilities, without regard for consequences.

Kia was very angry that Molowia had refused to continue training her, just for wanting to help her family. She had never understood Molowia's determination to remain neutral. Kia was angry at being treated like a child. She seethed with resentment at being prevented from living up to her full potential.

But that didn't matter now. Molowia was no longer necessary. Kia didn't need a mortal teacher any longer. Molowia had never reached the levels where Kia was traversing. Kia had moved far beyond her teacher. She was beyond being just a simple shaman, and so needed a teacher who was more than a shaman.

Shula-Witsa had secret knowledge Molowia had never even conceived of. Surely a being of elemental fire could teach her miracles to astonish even Molowia herself. It was time for her to become the ultimate sorcerer.

Kia rarely slept anymore. She didn't seem to need much rest any longer. Something about this new power flowering within her allowed Kia to practice for days and not feel fatigued. The primal, eldritch energy that consumed her was intoxicating and addicting.

More! I must learn more!

Agwara the Snow Fox Spirit was making paw prints in the dirt. The creature had the ability to slightly alter its shape, and cunningly it made its own paws look like the paws of Lucifee the Wildcat. Agwara was smugly satisfied at his bit of chicanery. *Fool the Itiwana, this will.*

Agwara continued making paw prints until he reached the lake, Cle-Elum, which was the home of the creature that Agwara wanted Pahana to meet.

Die for certain Pahana will, when arrive he does, Agwara thought.

Only minutes later, a very confident Pahana came riding into view, with Chybiabis still close behind. Pahana was completely focused on the tracks, determined to locate and destroy the wildcat.

"These are fresh tracks, Chybiabis," he said. "Very fresh. I swear, we're close. We'll get him today, I'll wager."

The wolf growled as if in understanding of the comment. The animal followed along behind his master until they reached the lake, Cle-Elum. Pahana was perplexed to see that the tracks stopped at the water's edge.

"Well, this makes little sense, Chybiabis," he said. "I've never heard of Lucifee going for a swim. I thought the creature hated water. Curse his fanged face. He continues to vex me."

As Pahana put a foot in the muddy water to get a better look at what lurked under the surface, he fired an arrow randomly into the water, hoping to provoke a response. Could the wildcat be swimming unseen in this lake?

A large claw popped abruptly out of the lake and clamped onto Pahana's ankle. The Itiwana clan elder-son cried out as the colossal claw grabbed him tightly.

Up from the murky water rose a huge and hideous crab. It was the size of a bison, with terrifyingly large claws. Its black, unblinking eyes sat on foot-long stalks flanked by a pair of feelers. Pahana had never before felt the fear he experienced when the monstrous crab arose. In a panic, he tried to free his ankle, but the beast had an unshakably powerful grip.

"Ti-fear me-Typhion." the creature roared. "Ti-bleed-Typhion."

CHAPTER FOURTEEN

"Ti-perish-Typhion!" the monster howled chillingly.

Ti-Typhion, Pahana thought fearfully. He knew the legends of the deadly hermit crab king. Ti-Typhion was another poshayanki, who had served the Sky Elders in previous war. The crab king was now apparently on the side of Malsumis and the Enemy Way. Or perhaps it just wanted to kill any human that crossed its path.

"Ti-suffer-Typhion," it growled. "Ti-die-Typhion."

Chybiabis leaped, snarling savagely, attacking the crab king. The wolf locked its jaws around one of the crab's legs. With its other claw, Ti-Typhion grabbed Chybiabis by the scruff of the neck and tossed the canine away.

This distraction gave Pahana the time to put an arrow in his bow. He fired at the massive crab, but the shaft bounced off the crustacean's rock-hard shell.

World Giant charged to its master's rescue, bucking at the giant crab wildly. The crab's shell was unbroken, but the power of the big bison staggered the crab enough that it released Pahana and focused its attention on World Giant.

"Ti-Challenge-Typhion. Ti-destroy-Typhion."

The giant crustacean grabbed World Giant by the horns. The two titans wrestled briefly until Ti-Typhion began dragging World Giant into the lake. The bison resisted, but the poshayanki was so strong it managed to pull World Giant into the lake.

"No!" Pahana cried, firing another arrow, which did as little damage as the first one. He could only watch helplessly as World Giant was dragged down under the water. He didn't come back up.

"Curse your eyes, monster!" he shouted at the lake, furious at the loss of his loyal mount. "I'm going to come back here and catch you in my net and drag you to the biggest fire I can build and cook you alive, you ugly beast! I will make you regret you even saw me or my mount."

"Easy be won't that," a male voice said.

Pahana turned and saw the seven masked men staring at him. The painted masks mimicked the expressions of happiness, sadness, anger, fear, confusion, amazement, and contemplation. He knew instantly who they were. His father had told him this story several times. It was one of his favorite tales growing up, and he'd asked Tawa to repeat it many times. He particularly enjoyed that they spoke backward. These were the Koyamishi Mudheads.

"Should I be honored or worried?" Pahana asked as Chybiabis growled at them.

"Kill to easy isn't king crab," the Mudhead with the contemplation mask said. "Weapon powerful a without not."

"A powerful weapon?" Pahana repeated, focusing on that part of the sentence. "A weapon I can use to kill creatures like Ti-Typhion and A'Chiyala and Lucifee? A weapon that will help the Itiwana against the villains of the Enemy Way? Speak to me."

"Manabazo by here sent were we," the happy-face Mudhead said. "You help to want we."

"Manabazo sent you here to check on me?" Pahana asked. "It was probably my grandmother's idea. She doesn't trust my friend Hayoka."

"Test our pass must you," the anger-faced Mudhead added.

"I expected a test," Pahana said, boldly. "Go on then. Do your worst."

The Mudhead with the sad-faced mask stood before Pahana and stared at him. Pahana immediately felt total despair. All the sadness in the world piled upon him. His mind went beyond morose and was buried in a sea of depression.

He wanted to crawl away and find a hole to die in because everything seemed so hopeless.

Pahana knew, however, he couldn't let himself submit. His father had not allowed himself to be broken by the Mudheads years ago, and so neither would Pahana. The thought of his father brought inspiration and courage to him.

"I will not humiliate my clan," he yelled. "I am not deterred. I will continue onward."

Finally, the wave of sadness ceased. Pahana exhaled, very relieved the assault was over. The Mudheads all nodded in unison.

"Passed have you," the contemplative Mudhead said.

"Good," Pahana said, still flummoxed by the experience. "Now, tell me where I can find this weapon?"

Hayoka was talking to Dagwona, the Whirlwind Witch, on a secluded path in the woods. Despite her odd way of talking, he found himself enjoying the conversation with her. Aside from being a unique and interesting woman, she had an enticing sexual quality.

"You're the second of your kind to contact me," Hayoka said, sitting on his bison. "Agwara came to me earlier."

"Agwara's an ally also," Dagwona said. "Itiwana isn't. Arrogant ants. Such scheming snakes. Ultimately unkind."

"I am keeping cautious," Hayoka said. "I've been warned about them. But I haven't seen…"

"Don't distrust Dagwona," she insisted. "Dagwona's dependable. Helping Hayoka. Itiwana isn't. Pahana poisonous. He'll hurt Hayoka. Remain ready. Always alert."

"I'll stay alert," he said. "But you said you have answers to my questions about 'coyote?'"

"Answers await. Patience, please."

"If I must wait, I will," Hayoka said. "I anticipate that it will be worth it."

"Smartly said," she told him. She came closer to the bison and reached up, pulling Hayoka's face nearer to hers. Surprisingly, she kissed him. "Hayoka's handsome."

"Oh, well, thank you," he replied awkwardly. "You're a pleasant sight, too."

She grinned seductively. "Dagwona departs. She'll see smart soul soon."

Hayoka watched as another gust of wind came and carried Dagwona away. He hoped he'd see her again. He liked her, and he wanted the answers she had. As he mused over what she'd said, Pahana came into view, walking with his wolf at his side. Hayoka acted casual, hoping Pahana hadn't heard the wind gusts.

"Where's your mount?" Hayoka asked.

"That tale is woeful," Pahana said. "I will explain in time, but for the moment, a new quest spurs me on. I prefer to think of adventure instead."

"What adventure would that be?" Hayoka inquired.

"A chance to gain a weapon that would give us an advantage against our enemies," Pahana replied. "Come; let us mount your bison. Gray Shadow will have two riders. We'll talk on the way. I still expect this trip to end in glory."

The wounded Tawa and his mount had crossed the Great Waters of the north again and were making their way across land. Tawa sat unsteadily atop his mount, feeling increasingly weak and sick.

It was getting colder, and he had lost a lot of blood. The Itiwana kik-mongwi looked at the infected wound, which had become swollen and inflamed. He didn't understand why he was feeling so drained of life. Tawa was beginning to doubt that he would reach his beloved Shipapa-Lina.

I fear I'm dying, he thought with dread, wondering what would happen to his people should he fall. Would he die alone, so far from home?

CHAPTER FIFTEEN

Pahana and Hayoka rode overnight to reach the location that the Koyamishi Mudheads had directed him to. It was called the Bitter Root Valley, home of the Puk-Wudjies.

Hayoka directed big Gray Shadow across a field while Pahana sat behind him, giving directions. Pahana had been to the Bitter Root Valley once before. He and his father had traveled there in an ill-fated attempt to form an alliance with the Puk-Wudjies, hoping to recruit them to fight the Tunerak Destroyers and the Skinwalkers. They discovered that the Puk-Wudjies are not hospitable hosts.

Pahana was telling Hayoka about his previous visit to the valley. "These Puk-Wudjies are a strange and wild tribe. They are all dwarves with a repulsive appetite for human flesh."

"Man-eating dwarves?"

"They are as disturbing as they sound," Pahana replied. "I had barely reached manhood when I last traveled here with my father. Chybiabis here was just a pup. We tried to secure their assistance against the Enemy Way but were set upon the moment we arrived. It's surprising how formidable such little people can be. There were enough of us to fight our way out, but it was an unpleasant visit overall."

Hayoka was beginning to get very nervous about this visit. "Need I say that there are only two of us? I know you enjoy a fight, but doesn't the idea of being eaten by cannibal dwarves make you want to get help before you attempt this?"

"I'm honored by your concern for me," Pahana said. "Truly I am."

"I'm also somewhat concerned that they'll destroy me along with you," Hayoka added.

"We're not going to be destroyed, my friend. Trust in me."

Minutes later, Hayoka spotted a valley and pointed. "Is that our destination?"

"Ah, excellent. We're here." Pahana said. "The Bitter Root Valley."

"And have you a plan in mind for obtaining this weapon without our being devoured by flesh-eating little men?" Hayoka asked.

Pahana looked surprisingly calm. "All it takes is a little bit of intelligence. And a distraction."

Calian rode swiftly atop Walking Storm, trying his best to catch up with Pahana. He had been given permission by Atira to catch up with the clan elder-son once his morning duties were done. She told him to be sure he found Pahana. Calian vowed he would. The clever tracker picked up a trail near the lake, surprised at seeing the buffalo tracks lead into the water but not out. Calian feared the worst until he found the tracks of the other bison nearby. On closer look, he realized that the second set of bison's paw prints were deeper, heading away from the lake.

It had two riders when it left, he thought. *So only a bison was killed here. What could have done it?* Calian thought.

He noticed some bubbling coming from the lake. Whatever was causing those bubbles was large. It may have been large enough to drown a bison. Calian cautiously backed away from the water. *Whatever it is, I leave it dominion of the lake.*

Calian rode off on the trail of Pahana, who was long overdue for his return. He was only meant to be gone for the morning. Both his mother and grandmother were very concerned. They knew Calian was the one to find him.

Calian, always a smart fellow, brought some powerful assistance with him. Faw-Faw, the Wood Man, ran alongside the bison. Calian had no idea what sort of danger they would run into, so he brought the strongest fighter of the tribe with him. Faw-Faw was always very protective of Calian, having been so close to his father, Pogum. It was easy to persuade the big, hairy man to accompany him. It would, in fact, have been hard to convince him to remain behind.

Calian didn't sleep and continued tracking Pahana overnight. In the morning, he held up a hand, signaling Faw-Faw to stop. "Slow your stride, old friend," he said as he hopped off his mount.

Faw-Faw watched as Calian kneeled and examined the dirt. He closely studied some paw tracks and determined that they were the prints of Gray Shadow.

"Still only one trail, Faw-Faw," he said. "I can't see any sign of World Giant. Where could they be headed? I must find them in case that wretched Hayoka is scheming something. Is he taking Pahana into a trap? He'd best pray Pahana is with him when I reach them. If not, I will forcefully ask him where Pahana is. And if he refuses to say, you and I will spend many hours thrashing him until he sings the song we want to hear."

"Gug," Faw-Faw grunted.

Calian leaped back onto Walking Storm. "Come, good friend. Let's find our clan elder-son."

Pahana and Hayoka approached a small brook not far from the mouth of a cave. Pahana got down on one knee and gazed into the water. "This is how my father escaped on that last visit."

Hayoka was confused. "I have no doubt that I am extremely stupid, but all I see is a brook."

"You are half correct," Pahana said, dipping his fingers in the water. "My father was separated from the rest of the war party. He tried to win us some additional time to escape from the caves below. He seemed to be trapped below but fell into an underground grotto. There he found a water-filled tunnel, and this is where he came out. I clearly remember him rising from this brook like a breaching whale to the delight of the rest of us. His discovery is how I'll get in. I simply need you to attract their attention."

"Why do I feel that I will not like this idea?"

Kia enjoyed the fact that she was moving beyond her physical limitations as a mortal girl. Her power consistently kept increasing. She was intoxicated by the uncanny energy which was transforming her. She was no longer the person she had been days earlier. *Amazing. Wonderful! I want more!*

She wished she could show off her new skills to Molowia and prove that the old shaman had sorely underestimated her. She resisted this urge, however, because Molowia might still be able to slow her progress, and Kia would not allow that.

Gazing into the abyss, Kia let out an excited giggle of jubilation. She drifted through the dark, dreamlike spirit realm like a fearless invader. Kia could not take her eyes off the astonishing, bewildering vistas strewn throughout these alternate worlds. She could not understand what she was seeing, but that didn't frighten her. Kia was determined to bend whatever creatures dwelled within those strange realms to her will. She would tame them, whatever they were. She would master the unreal reality of the spirit realm, transforming it into her personal domain. She was obsessed with becoming the chieftain of this fantastic world and using it as a place to launch attacks against the Enemy Way.

I will overcome this mystery realm, and the Enemy Way will rue the day.

CHAPTER SIXTEEN

Pahana and Hayoka stood in the mouth of the cave. Hayoka was not optimistic about this strategy. "You're certain this is the proper cave?"

"I am," Pahana said. "My visit here is carved in my memory. It is not an easy day to forget."

"And you'll not reconsider this plan?"

"Never reconsider a good plan," Pahana said with unflinching confidence.

Pahana kneeled and touched the floor of the cave. He willed his inner power as the son of an artic goddess to be unleashed. Ice spread from his fingers, creeping across the stone surface. He froze a section of the cave.

Smiling, Pahana headed to the brook. "Indicate to me when they are coming, and I'll begin my aquatic incursion."

Hayoka gave a less-than-enthusiastic nod. Stepping into the cave, careful not to slip on the ice, Hayoka unleashed a loud, whooping cry, which echoed through the underground caves. At first, there was no response, so he continued to make as much noise as possible. He yelled for several minutes until he got the attention he desired.

At first, he wasn't sure if he actually saw something moving in the darkness or if it was a trick of his imagination. Then, however, he heard something moving. After that, the inhabitants of that dark place stepped out of the shadows and into full view.

The Puk-Wudjies were only waist-high to Hayoka, and he was not particularly tall himself. Their skulls seemed to be disproportionately large in comparison to the rest of their bodies, and the eyes seemed small, as if withered by lack of use. Their ears were large since they used sound as their guide rather than vision. The most disturbing thing about them was that their teeth were rows of knife-like fangs, evolved from generations of carnivorous feeding.

Hayoka took a few steps backward, out of the cave, until he was visible to Pahana. Behind his back, he made a gesture. Pahana saw the signal and dived into the brook. Skimming along the bottom, Pahana found the submerged tunnel his father had once used. He hoped he could hold his breath long enough to reach the other end. His father had once done it, and so he told himself he must do it, too.

Back in the cave, the Puk-Wudjies made a sound that resembled a cross between a hiss and a squeal. The little carnivores had cougars with them, bound by rope-like leashes. The cougars roared at the intruder, obviously eager for the kill. The Puk-Wudjies muttered something that Hayoka could not quite make out, followed by them releasing one of the cougars. The cat sprinted toward Hayoka with terrible intentions. Hayoka turned and ran for his life.

As Hayoka raced away from the cave, the cougar tried to leap out of the cave mouth to pounce on him, but the big cat slipped on the ice. The cat slid but didn't fall. It regained its footing and ran to catch up with Hayoka. However, before it reached him, it was interrupted by a fiercer adversary.

Chybiabis leaped into the cougar's path. The cougar came to a stop as the wolf snarled ferociously at him. There was a tense standoff between the two creatures. Each tried to intimidate the other into backing down. When the cougar did not retreat, Chybiabis responded by lunging forward. The cougar swatted at the wolf, but Chybiabis ferociously bit the cougar's leg. They scuffled, clawing at each other. Teeth and claws slashed as they rolled across the ground.

It was Chybiabis who backed away first, but the cat was not yet done. It lashed out with its front legs and deadly claws. The wolf retaliated with powerful bites that injured the cougar. Despite the cougar's superior size, the wolf's stamina and fierce loyalty to the Itiwana became a factor. When the cougar got tired, the tide turned. Realizing it was in grave danger, the cougar retreated back into the cave. Chybiabis howled a victory howl.

"Good wolf," Hayoka said, relieved.

His relief faded when the cougar returned with reinforcement. Three other cougars had been loosed to deal with the wolf. Chybiabis backed off, sensing the danger, while Hayoka looked for a place to hide.

However, the Itiwana had one more ally. Gray Shadow was spooked by the approaching cats and took up a defensive position. When the big bison stomped toward them, the cougars all turned tail and retreated. Gray Shadow and Chybiabis chased the cougars back into the cave.

The Itiwana choose their animals well, Hayoka thought.

There was nothing Hayoka could do now except wait. He had created the distraction that Pahana wanted, and now it was up to the clan elder-son to find the mysterious weapon he had come for.

As Kia continued to excitedly explore the strange spirit world, she heard other voices in that unreal place. Voices of men. Voices seeking a language she could understand. This was not the voice of Shula-Witsa. Clearly, there are other beings residing within that odd world. Other minds reached out to her, caressing her questing brain, letting her know she was not alone in that place of mystery.

Kia experienced things she could not imagine, and she wanted to know more. She would not be denied. Whatever secrets lurked there, she was going to uncover them. Kia pushed past her fears and doubts. *I have no reason to be afraid. I am too powerful.*

Kia pushed her way beyond the preternatural veil. The young girl broke past that supernatural barrier from which other mortals, including Molowia, had been repeatedly turned back. It was considered unbreachable.

Kia shattered the wall between magical lands, forcing her way into a surreal new domain of gods and spirits and demons and monsters. It was a place where even kachinas and poshayankis would tread carefully.

The otherworldly place drew her in irresistibly. Heart racing with excitement, she used her astral form to examine this new world. She invaded the spirit kingdom fearlessly. Kia should have been afraid, but she wasn't. If Molowia had been there with her, she would have warned Kia to be cautious. But that didn't matter to Kia. Not now. Kia was not going to allow fear to stop her from experiencing the glory of this. She continued to push onward across this numinous realm, determined to become queen of whatever lay beyond.

Kia kept searching for the source of those voices. The utterances became clearer and more distinct. As her astral form moved through the foggy realm, the voices became louder. She was determined to see who was speaking.

She succeeded in locating the area from where those voices originated. Kia saw numerous strange life forms, many of which she didn't recognize. Others who walked within this marshy world were familiar, like mortal men. Some of them seemed to be oblivious or uncaring regarding the presence of these monstrous creatures, while other human-like warriors were in battle against these horrid beasts.

Her attention was drawn to one particular man. He seemed to be a man very much like her own people. The sight of this man made her think of an image she'd seen somewhere before but couldn't exactly recall from where. *How do I know that face?*

That lean, handsome man with some slight scarring across his body was fighting a saber-toothed, goat-like beast with three horns. The man fought valiantly, using a spear and shield. His boldness and daring were most impressive. The man's valiant efforts were pushing the beast back, but the animal made one final attempt to pierce the man with its horns. Luckily, the agile man evaded the attack and jabbed the large goat with his spear. The goat bleated in agony and collapsed. The man took a moment to compose himself and then pulled out his spear.

"That was for the Itiwana," he said as he stepped casually over the body, which was rapidly devoured by tiny, carnivorous creatures who feasted on the defeated.

Kia overheard what the man had said and was amazed. Who was this person skulking beyond the veil, fighting evil spirits and demons in the name of the Itiwana? What was he doing there? What was his purpose? Why was this brave warrior battling impossible beasts in this hidden realm? Why would a man separated from the mortal world speak of his fealty to the Itiwana? She watched curiously as the man locked in battle with a second monstrous foe.

He didn't seem to know she was there. At least, not yet. She could hear him, but he did not hear her. She saw him, but he did not see her. Her invisible astral form moved in closer to the battle, watching him batter and wound his foe with impressive skill until the strange beast slinked away in defeat, vanishing into the dark nothingness. The fearless man seemed almost sad that he had to injure and kill these opponents, but once again said, "For the Itiwana."

Kia was very curious about this apparently normal man who seemed reluctant to kill and yet seemed so willing to do so in the name of her own people. Now, more than ever, she wanted to know more about him. What connection did he have to the Itiwana?

She tried to speak to him, but she couldn't communicate. She yelled to get his attention, but it did no good. She could only watch the warrior wander the nebulous landscape, along with other strange, shadowy figures. Some of the other human-like men acknowledged him respectfully, while others seemed intimidated by him. The man seemed to walk through this strange realm with a confident pride in himself that was enviable. There was something special about this mystery man. She had to learn what he was doing here in this unfathomable place.

She continued to observe him stalking other hideous creatures, all of whom gave him a wide berth. They feared him. Something about this man was indefatigable. He would not quit, no matter what menace confronted him. He faced down these strange creatures of the other world, who seemed no match for his skill, his speed, his courage, and his determination.

No new challengers came forward. It seemed as if some rest period had silently been called. The chatter of background voices continued, but no one was fighting. Confident that he had temporarily dominated the zone of battle, the mystery man sat down for a rest.

Kia didn't know if he had a normal, physical body as we know it. Yet, whether this was an astral form or an actual mortal body, it seemingly needed to be replenished. Or perhaps it was just a spiritual rest that he required. It was possible he was simply summoning up his will for the next battle. Or maybe he was remembering some other, better life that had been lost to him.

I must know more about this man, she thought. *I must speak to him.*

Her desire to meet and talk to him had an unexpected result. She suddenly felt a tingling sensation, which confused her because she was not in her mortal body. She realized that a new body had manifested where her astral form had been. She had solid limbs. Kia raised her arms to look at her physical hands. She wriggled her fingers, perplexed. She felt breath and a heartbeat. She felt everything that a human body would normally feel.

How did this happen? she wondered. *I didn't know I had this power. Now I can participate in events.*

Now that she was standing in this realm on two feet, she opened her mouth to speak. On her first try, nothing came out. But on her second attempt, she found her voice. "Hello."

She walked toward this mysterious man. At first, he gave her only a casual glance, but then he raised his eyebrows and fixed his gaze upon her, as if he'd just noticed something. He rose and walked toward her, studying Kia curiously.

"You don't belong here," the man said. "This is no place for you. You are not like the rest of us. You were not a spirit; you came here. You were alive. How did you get here?"

Kia reached out to touch him. Putting her palm on his chest, she noted that he felt solid. She still wondered what was so familiar about him.

"You're right. I am not dead," she said. "I am a shaman. I have willed myself into this world because I sensed you. I heard your voice. I wanted to know more about you."

"Me?" he asked. "I'm simply a spirit wandering between realms."

"But you came from my world, didn't you?" she asked.

"I did," the man answered. "But I have chosen to remain a sentry at this gateway between the human world and the dread realm of the beasts. I have foresworn myself to spend my afterlife protecting Ulah-Nane from creatures who would cross over from the transcendent, secret places beyond imagination. These creatures would dare to walk into the fair world of my birth. Such monsters are powerful and unpredictable and may cause havoc at a time when a war of gods is already causing too much strife. I will not let them pass! I cannot stop them all, but I will stop as many as I can. One day I may fall, but until then, I will continue with this battle. I will protect not only the Itiwana, but all mortals. While I am in this realm, I will not rest until the God War is ended."

"I am very impressed," Kia said. "Such raw courage. I didn't know there were such people as you, other than my father. You remind me of him. I've met many determined warriors, but your devotion goes beyond even them. Perhaps I've spent too much time studying as a shaman in Kolhu, and I've been too sheltered."

"Kolhu?" the man asked. "The sister city to my once-time home in Shipapa-Lina. Who are your parents? Perhaps I know them?"

She smiled proudly and announced, "My father is Tawa, chieftain of the Itiwana tribe. My mother is Pinga, the former Sky Elder. I am their youngest child. My name is Kia."

Gladdened by this information, the warrior leaned forward to get a better look at her face. "Ah yes, I see the resemblance now. I should have known by the snowy whiteness of your hair that you were kin of Pinga. I see the eyes of Tawa on your youthful face, Kia. I had once devoted myself to him, as I did to his father before him. He is a good man."

"Yes, he's a great man," she added. "He rules our people well."

"Good," the mysterious warrior replied with a weary smile. "It is good to know that after all these years, he's still defending his people. I would expect nothing less."

"He's been away on a mission of late," Kia said. "I don't know what his condition is just now, and I worry for him. My brother Pahana is leading the Itiwana tribe. The descendants of Morning Star are still the rulers of Shipapa-Lina, and I have been sent to Kolhu to study under Molowia. I was meant to become a shaman and to be Molowia's successor."

"Quite an honor," the unnamed man said. "Molowia is a great woman."

Kia didn't reply to the comment about Molowia, who she was angry with. She deftly changed the subject. "We all do our part in the war of Sky Elders. Aholi now commands the Two Horn Riders."

"Does he indeed?" the mysterious warrior said wistfully. "I had that honor once. Much has happened since I left. I wish I could go back to Shipapa-Lina. My soul forever yearns to see my own loved ones."

"Who are you?" Kia asked. "Maybe I know your name. Something about you seems familiar to me."

He looked dreamily into the misty darkness. "My name is Pogum."

CHAPTER SEVENTEEN

Pahana had never thought that air could be so wonderful. He had felt his lungs were going to burst like insects coming out of an egg sack. When he broke the surface, he thanked Awona'Wilona for the air he breathed.

What he was vexed about was the total darkness. He hadn't anticipated that. The last time he was in these caves, there were torches lit. It hadn't occurred to him that those were only for the benefit of the Itiwana, to lure them into a sense of comfort before the trap was sprung. Pahana hadn't considered that the Puk-Wudjies themselves needed no light. They had developed a way of using their hearing to navigate the darkness.

Pahana stumbled in the darkness, feeling around for the weapon that the Mudheads had spoken of. He knew what size and shape it was and what it was made of. Also, he was certain that as soon as he touched it, he would instinctively know what it was since it was used by his ancestor, Morning Star. All he needed to do was touch it. He hoped he could find it in the dark before the Puk-Wudjies returned.

But it was not to be. He felt a forceful and painful blow to the side of his head, and that was the last thing he knew for a while.

Sometime later, Pahana awoke. His head was throbbing, but he was more concerned about his restraints. Someone had bound him while he was unconscious. He was restrained by something similar to snake skins. He could not free himself.

One small relief for Pahana was that there was now some light in the cave coming from an open flame. He wondered what the purpose of the fire was. His heart sank when he saw several Puk-Wudgies standing around a huge, reddish-brown clay pot. Under the pot was the flame from where that light was coming. He sensed that this was not going to be pleasant for him.

One of the Puk-Wudjies turned his attention to Pahana. His grin was unnerving. "Welcome to our home, intruder. Enjoy your precious moments here, because they are few and dwindling rapidly."

"Why am I bound?" Pahana asked, sounding as angry as possible. "Who are you?"

"I am Mikum-Wesu, High Master of the Black Tamanus council and ruler of the Puk-Wudjies. And as for why you are bound, it is dirt simple. We're merely waiting until the water boils, and then you'll be dropped inside. Your death by boiling will be quite painful, but that is the punishment for intruding where you have not been welcomed. Afterward, the Black Tamanus council will have a good meal. That meal, if you have not yet guessed, is you."

"My name is Pogum," the brave warrior said. "I am kin to your father and therefore kin to you, as well. We are family, Kia."

Kia's face brightened in amazement. "Pogum! The great hero of legend? You're the man so often spoken about? You are revered among the Itiwana as the first leader of the Two-Horn Riders. Every child among the Itiwana knows the story of how you sacrificed yourself to destroy the Wendigo. My father describes you as one of the greatest men he's ever known. You have not been forgotten."

Chuckling, Pogum tapped his fingers against his shield. "Thank you for that information, Kia. It's touching to hear that my people still remember me. I certainly remember them. I think about them constantly, especially my dear wife, Bluebird, the Blue Corn Maiden. How is she?"

"Very well, the last time I saw her," Kia replied.

"And what of my child?" he asked. "Bluebird was to have a child when I was killed. Did she?"

"She did," Kia said, glad to be the bearer of this good news. "You have a son. His name is Calian. I haven't seen him in a long time, because I've been away, but I understand he's a very strong and very intelligent man. He is a close friend to my brother."

A wide grin crossed Pogum's haggard face. "This is wonderful," Pogum said. "Ah, a son. This makes me very happy, Kia. What better news could a father and husband have than to hear that his wife and son still thrive? That they're happy."

Kia, being very young, didn't know whether she should tell him that his family had been happy without him or that they were sad because they missed him so much. *What's the right thing to say?*

"Bluebird is a good mother," she told him. "She's been very strong for her son. Calian looks very much like you. He and Pahana are bonded like brothers."

"Of course," Pogum said proudly. "That's how it should be. The son of Tawa and the son of Pogum, forever guarding the city of Shipapa-Lina together. That is the proper way of destiny. Thank you for telling me all this."

As Pogum beamed with melancholy pride, Kia was distracted by unnerving, inexplicable sounds in the distance. These sounds filled her with intense anxiety.

"One more question, if I may?" Pogum asked. "Did the Itiwana ever learn what the three omens of Malsumis were?"

Kia knew about the three omens well. Everyone among the Itiwana did. Years ago, Pogum had learned that three unspecified omens would signal the resurrection of Malsumis. No one, not even Manabazo, had been able to explain what those portents could be. "I regret to say no."

"That's a dour bit of news," Pogum said with a resigned sigh.

Kia could no longer wait to discuss her own agenda. "Now, maybe you can help me. I need something from you."

"Ah, of course," he said. "Why are you here, girl? I ask, what purpose do you have in this dark, dismal place?"

"I was about to ask you the same thing, Pogum," she said. "How did you come to be here?"

Pogum tapped his spear against the peaty ground. "Because this is where I should be. As I told you before, I chose to be in this place. I could have gone to my rest in the holy hunting ground, but I knew the war of the Sky Elders was still raging. I knew that Shipapa-Lina and the Itiwana were in danger. How could I allow my soul to go to rest eternally when I knew that my wife, my child, my chieftain, and my people were under siege? Given the option of selfish peace or endless battle, I thought about my village, and the answer was easy. The danger to my loved ones could not be ignored. I could not go to rest knowing Shipapa-Lina might fall in my absence. And so, my soul implored one of the Sky Elders, Great Manitou, to allow me to help."

"You ... spoke to Manitou?" Kia asked, stunned.

"I did," he told her. "I asked him if I could still play a part in this war. Due to their godly conflict, Manitou gladly permitted me to continue serving, even after my death. He sent me here to this realm between realms—to this barrier between worlds, where monsters come to make their way from the dark chasm of mystery and join the Enemy Way. If allowed to breach the barrier, they will cause bedlam in the mortal realm. Therefore, it is here that I stand as the chief defender of all mortals, no matter who they worship. And I will continue to fight until I fall."

"But how can you die?" she asked. "I mean, you are already dead, aren't you?"

"I am," he said. "My current state is ... different. I am something in between life and death. I am part soul and part substance. I can feel pain and I can get tired. This surrogate body can be destroyed. The body you currently inhabit is the same."

Kia looks at her hands again. "I can be hurt? Killed? Thank you for warning me."

"It is the gift of Manitou," Pogum said. "This place grants anyone with great strength of will the ability to form a solid spirit body. This body I inhabit has been pummeled and battered worse than my original scarred body ever was. Some creatures have fought their way past me, despite my best efforts to stop them. One of them almost destroyed this body. One day I will likely fall and be forced to return to the holy hunting ground. When this happens, at least I'll know I did my best for my people. I died for their protection, and my soul continued in their service as long as possible. I will rest better for this."

The roar of another unseen beast was heard nearby. "Excuse me, Kia. I am needed. Something needs to be killed."

CHAPTER EIGHTEEN

Pahana struggled desperately against his bonds but could not get free. He tried to remain calm, but that was difficult under the circumstances. The Puk-Wudjies were serious about wanting to consume him. He knew their carnivorous habits well from his past experience with them. His mind whirled with desperate ideas about how to escape his imminent doom.

Mikum-Wesu displayed his fanged incisors in a satisfied smirk as he looked at the flames. "Ah, the sensation of a scorching fire. Big enough to roast a pig. Lovely, isn't it?"

"Your pardon if I do not share your enthusiasm," Pahana answered with all the boldness he could muster.

"Ha! I like a man who dies well," Mikum-Wesu said. "I suspect the water will be sufficiently heated now. I do so enjoy the sound of boiling water, don't you? There will be excellent eating tonight, I predict."

Mikum-Wesu waved for several of the other Puk-Wudjies to join him. "It's time to move this invader to the cauldron."

Pahana was slowly starting to wriggle his way loose from his bonds, but he needed more time. He wished for a distraction until he could escape.

"Wait a moment," Pahana said. "How is it that you know the Old Speak of the ancient chieftains? The last time I was here..."

"We've known the Old Speak for very many seasons," Mikum-Wesu answered. "We simply choose not to speak to outsiders. We were taught the language by Kukwis, the man-eating ogre. If you do not know of Kukwis, he is one of the Cheenook giants."

"As the Wendigo are?" Pahana asked.

"I don't know of these Wendigo, but I know that there are many types of Cheenook," Mikum-Wesu replied. "Our experiences with mighty Kukwis go back many years. My ancestors bore witness when Kukwis first came to the Bitter Root Valley, wounded in a battle against a servant of Awona'Wilona named Morning Star."

Pahana did not mention his relation to the revered Morning Star. "And you didn't eat him? Were your ancestors fasting at the time?"

"Our people do not eat Cheenooks," Mikum-Wesu said. "We see the value in having them as allies. He generously gave us a sacred weapon as a gift."

"A weapon?" Pahana asked, wondering if it was the same one he had come looking for. "What weapon was this?"

"The sacred, invincible tomahawk of Awona'Wilona," Mikum-Wesu said as the slavering Puk-Wudjies circled him. "Kukwis got it from Agwara, who had stolen it from the human tribe that slew Shakok. When the weapon was used on Kukwis, he asked Agwara to steal it away. After we nursed him, Kukwis gave the tomahawk to us in gratitude."

"I see," Pahana said. "But..."

"But enough of this pointless discussion," Mikum-Witsu snapped. "It shouldn't concern you. You're only purpose now is to be a tasty meal."

At Mikum-Wesu's command, a group of Puk-Wudjies gathered around Pahana to untie him from the stake and move him into the cauldron.

Hayoka waited outside the cave, pensively pacing. He wondered what could be happening inside those ominous caves. Had Pahana found the thing he was looking for? Had he been discovered? Had he even made it out of the watery tunnel? Was he alive? Hayoka wondered what to do now. *Should I go in there to see if he needs help?*

Hayoka chose not to attempt a rescue. He did not believe he could succeed and was unwilling to perform a suicidal attack. He decided to move farther away from the cave mouth, fearing that some of the Puk-Wudjies might emerge. Hayoka ducked into the bushes, where he could more easily flee if the enemies appeared.

No sooner had he found the proper place to conceal himself than a strong pair of hands grabbed him from behind. Hayoka was yanked backward and slammed to the ground. The back of his head hit the dirt. Hayoka was rattled by the impact. The wind had been knocked out of him and he looked up to see who his assailant was.

"Calian?" Hayoka gasped when he saw who it was.

Calian stood over Hayoka, stomping down a foot on Hayoka's chest. Hayoka winced as the foot slammed down on him. Calian sneered angrily down at Hayoka, pointing a spear at his neck.

"Where is Pahana?" Calian asked loudly. "And pray I like your answer."

Hayoka glared up at his main detractor, unhappy with being stomped on. "A polite query would have been sufficient. What are you doing here?"

"I tracked your mount," Calian snapped back. "Now answer the question before I summon my bison to stand on you. Where is Pahana?"

Hayoka pointed to the cave. "In there."

Calian studied the cave entrance but kept one eye on Hayoka. "What's he doing in there?"

Hayoka related the whole story of Ti-Typhion, the death of World Giant, the Mudheads, and the mysterious weapon. The only thing he left out was his meeting with Dagwona. Calian would not respond well to that.

"The last I saw of Pahana, he dived into that brook," Hayoka said. "Apparently, there is a tunnel that..."

"I know of it," Calian said. "I was here when Tawa used it."

"Of course you were," Hayoka said. "If Pahana was here, so were you. The faithful watchdog ever at his master's side. Might I suggest that you take that spear away from my throat so that we can focus our efforts on retrieving our imperiled friend from his present predicament?"

Calian allowed Hayoka to rise. Hayoka considered striking Calian in retaliation, but felt this wasn't the time for a fight. Aside from that, he saw big Faw-Faw standing nearby, watching them from behind a tree. He knew how loyal the Wood Man was and felt certain the huge man would pound him into the dirt should he dare accost Calian.

"We must go in there," Calian said. "Pahana may need us."

"We need to think this through carefully," Hayoka said. "Walking foolishly into their hands will not help Pahana. It will only add to the dwarves' meal."

Calian looked over the band of cohorts he had to work with. His allies were Faw-Faw, Chybiabis,

Walking Storm, Gray Shadow, and the untrust-worthy Hayoka. What sort of rescue could he mount with this motley lot?

"We should divide our forces," Calian said. "You'll challenge them directly with Faw-Faw and the animals. Get their attention. While they're dis-tracted, I'll go in through the underwater tunnel."

Hayoka shook his head. "Your thinking is flawed. Most likely because you don't do enough of it. You should practice more. Pahana tried exactly that tactic already and seemingly got caught. They'll be expecting a rescuer to do the same. We need to alter the strategy."

"I anxiously await your superior suggestion," Calian said sarcastically.

"I have one."

CHAPTER NINETEEN

After gathering up some useful items from the immediate area, Hayoka was ready to put his rescue plan into action. *I hope this works, or Calian will no doubt blame me. He and Faw-Faw will probably beat me to death.*

While Calian lit a small fire, Hayoka gathered up large, tumbling tangles of weeds. Faw-Faw found a thick, heavy log and easily carried it over his shoulder. After that, Hayoka spotted a big boulder and asked Calian to instruct Faw-Faw to push the boulder near the cave mouth. Walking Storm helped Faw-Faw push.

Everything was finally in place. The rescuers positioned the tangled weeds strategically at the cave mouth. Hayoka gestured toward the cave, indicating to Calian that it was time to start the rescue. Calian took a flaming stick from the fire and used it to set the tumbleweeds ablaze.

"Now Faw-Faw," Calian said. "Blow."

Faw-Faw took a deep breath, soaking as much air into his lungs as possible, and then let out a blast of oxygen toward the tumbleweeds. The weeds blew into the cave mouth, rolling down the incline toward the deeper regions where the inhabitants lurked.

A dozen Puk-Wudjies had untied Pahana from the stake. They were slowly dragging the thrashing and flailing Itiwana warrior toward the boiling pot. They were having a very difficult time pulling him across the short distance because Pahana struggled so fiercely. However, the Puk-Wudjies had a considerable advantage in number. Also, Pahana's wrists were still bound together, limiting his offense. Despite his desperate struggle, his captors were slowly lugging him toward the fire and the cauldron.

The struggle was interrupted when the flaming tumbleweeds rolled into the den of the Mikum-Wesu. The startled Puk-Wudjies paused, distracted by the unexpected occurrence. The flaming balls ignited some cave weeds, as well as the hay and grass beddings that the Puk-Wudjies used. Smoke began to fill the cave, making it harder for the Puk-Wudjies to breathe. Also, the flame was agitating the cougars, who were tied to a post. They began to roar and wildly squirm in an attempt to break their restraints.

The Puk-Wudjies had to concentrate first on putting the fires out. After that, they heard several loud footsteps coming down the outer cave slope into their lair. Big Faw-Faw came charging in, carrying a large log. Behind him were the two bison, as well as Chybiabis. The wolf howled in an intimidating manner.

The Puk-Wudjies immediately began their defensive measures. First, they released the cougars, although this tactic wasn't overly useful. The cougars were already frightened by the smoke and embers of flame. Additionally, they were not very effective against the bison. The cats backed away from the horned beasts. Chybiabis contributed by throwing himself into combat with the same cougar he'd fought earlier.

The Puk-Wudjies grabbed their slingshots, flinging rocks at Faw-Faw. The Wood Man used the log as a shield to protect himself. The rocks that did get past his defenses and impacted his hirsute body were quite painful to him. Yet he was too loyal to quit or retreat. The pain angered him, and an angry Wood Man was dangerous. Faw-Faw furiously battered many of them out of his way with the heavy log, which he swung with ease. The two bison also ignored the pain of the rocks and continued to rampage through the cave, causing chaos.

Pahana used the distraction to break away from the two Puk-Wudjies, who were still holding him. He proceeded to punch and kick at every Puk-Wudji who came within range of his fists. Despite the danger, some part of him enjoyed the melee. *By the gods, this is an adventure!*

Several Puk-Wudjis swarmed toward him, bearing their fangs and wielding small clubs. He prepared for the assault, but got some unexpected help. Calian popped up out of the underground stream and fired a few arrows at the Puk-Wudjies.

"Come," Calian yelled. "Hurry."

Pahana smiled and ran toward the pool, with Calian covering his escape. He leaped into the water. He and Calian vanished under the surface. Pahana led the retreat through the watery tunnel, followed closely by Calian.

Weakened from his experience and not having had the time to inhale deeply enough, Pahana ran out of air before he made it to the other end. He struggled to make it to the surface of the outside brook. Just short of the surface, he began to black out from lack of air. However, Calian—who was as good a swimmer as his father Pogum had been— grabbed his clan elder-son and dragged him to the surface. Pahana opened his mouth and devoured the delicious oxygen like a starving man.

Hayoka helped Calian pull Pahana out of the water. Pahana sat on the edge of the brook, breathing heavily. "Air is wonderful."

Calian let out a loud cry, which echoed into the cave. The sound of the call reached Faw-Faw and the animals. The animals were trained to respond to the call of an Itiwana, so they abandoned the battle and raced to answer Calian's call. Faw-Faw also heard the yell and followed the animals out.

The Wood Man, the two bison, and the wolf darted out of the cave. Calian ran to the boulder and signaled for Faw-Faw to join him. Together, they began pushing the boulder toward the cave. Hayoka led Walking Storm and Gray Shadow to the boulder. The two mounts helped push the rock.

The Puk-Wudjies were scrambling up the inner-cave incline, heading toward the sun and the open air. They reached the cave mouth in time to see a stone rolling across the cavern entrance. Calian and his team managed to push the big boulder in front of the opening, blocking it completely. There wasn't even enough space for one of the diminutive Puk-Wudjies to slip through.

Still disoriented, Pahana had enough mental wherewithal to stick his hand in the brook and use his divine power to chill the water. In moments, the whole brook froze into a solid block. *The damned creatures won't be able to pursue us that way.*

While Pahana took a deep breath to recover from his exertions and Calian kept a watchful eye on the bolder to be sure no enemies got through, Hayoka smirked at the success of his plan.

"Splendid," Hayoka said. "That went quite well, I think."

Pahana, having regained his senses, stood up and nodded approvingly at the others. "Well done indeed, good friends. You couldn't have pleased me better. And you, dear Calian, your arrival was fortuitous. I'm pleased you arrived when you did."

"Always at your pleasure, my clan elder-son."

"Quite a clever plan, Uncle."

Calian was loath to admit it was Hayoka who came up with the plan, but he was too honest to lie to his leader. He pointed to Hayoka. "The credit must go to the mind that spawned the plan."

Pahana patted Hayoka on the shoulder. "I knew you had the fire to be a Two Horn Rider. You make me proud. You both do. And you as well, Faw-Faw."

Chybiabis rubbed up against his master's leg. Pahana patted the wolf on the muzzle. "And not to forget you, my fierce friend."

"We should go quickly," Calian said. "They'll manage to move the boulder before long. We should not be here when they do."

"Always the wise one, aren't you, Uncle?" Pahana said. He looked back at the cave. "I am loath to leave without the weapon I came for, but I swear to Awona'Wilona I will return to reclaim it for the Itiwana. By the blood of my ancestor, I make that vow."

"We believe you will, but Calian is correct," Hayoka said. "We should be off."

"Indeed, let us away," Pahana ordered.

Pahana climbed on top of Gray Shadow, along with Hayoka. Hayoka beamed smugly at Calian because the clan elder-son had chosen to ride with him instead of Calian. The distrustful Calian narrowed his eyes and added one more thing to the list of offenses he would remember when the time came to settle things between them.

"We ride," Pahana yelled.

The two Bison and their three passengers headed back toward Shipapa-Lina, with Faw-Faw and Chybiabis on foot. By the time the Puk-Wudjies freed themselves, the Itiwana were long gone.

"We won't forget this!" Mikum-Wesu vowed. "There will come a time when we'll taste his flesh."

In the mystifying, otherworldly realm, Kia had watched while Pogum destroyed several fearsome monsters. After the latest battle, he sat breathlessly on an immense toadstool. He wiped a demon's slimy, green blood off his spear by dragging the point through the reddish dirt of the odd terrain.

"Pogum, I need your help," Kia said. "I came here to learn secrets that have been hidden from mortals. I want to increase my powers in order to battle the Winter Elders. You said you were able to communicate with the great Manitou. Can you help me speak to him?"

"You wish to speak to Manitou?" Pogum asked. "The second most powerful of all the summer Sky Elders?"

"I must!" she insisted. "I wish to know so much more. Shula-Witsa has taught me quite a lot, and I'm learning to become a great shaman, but if I could learn more, if my power could increase, I know I could defeat the servants of the Enemy Way."

Pogum folded his arms and looked at her apprehensively. "Shula-Witsa? He's a wily one and not always to be trusted. While he has a fierce loyalty to Awona'Wilona, and he will do anything to defeat the Enemy Way, he is also rather ruthless. He can be manipulative. Shula-Witsa is very cunning but sometimes a trickster. You should be wary of him. He has been known to use others, leaving them devastated afterward. I fear he may be using you."

"I don't believe that," Kia snapped, protesting a little too much. "We need more Sky Elders who have such devotion to the cause. Some of them, such as the White Buffalo Woman and others, will just come and go. They'll disappear without a word, and we won't hear from them for long periods of time. They won't get involved until it suits them. Shula-Witsa has promised me that he'll be ready whenever I need him. So far, he has kept that promise."

"That may well be," Pogum said. "I can't comment on what Shula-Witsa has done, but I suggest there is a reason why the other Elders, such as Kokopelli, appear so randomly. I've learned there are good reasons why Awona'Wilona has not declared open war on the Winter Elders. He knows better than to escalate the war when it can possibly be prevented by protecting the Tree of

Life. Shula-Witsa, on the other hand, has his own plots. He is too confident in his cunning machinations. I would not trust him."

Kia became defensive. "I am willing to take that chance. Whatever he wants me to do, I'll do. I just want to help my father and my brother. I'm trying to protect my family and my people. If Shula-Witsa can help me do so, then I will serve him in any way I can."

Pogum looked over his shoulder at a strange creature skittering by. He kept his guard up, but didn't seem overly alarmed by it. He turned his attention back to Kia, clearly uneasy about her decision.

"Be cautious, Kia," Pogum said. "The Sky Elders are not always what they seem. Remember, they are far beyond us. They think in ways we cannot understand. Sometimes they can be rather callous and cold. So please, Kia, always remember your original goals. When you are listening to Shula-Witsa, think very carefully about whatever he asks you to do. Are you serving your people, or are you serving only him?"

Locked in her self-justifying logic, Kia reflexively defended her choice. "It's all the same, isn't it, Pogum? Shula-Witsa and the summer Sky Elders are allies to the Itiwana. If I can destroy the Enemy Way, what difference does it make whether I fight in the name of Shipapa-Lina or Shula-Witsa? As long as I have the power to destroy our foes, those details are not important."

Pogum seemed bothered by this argument. "I knew a man named Hobomok once. He wanted to protect the Itiwana by becoming their leader. He felt he was the best man to fight the Enemy Way. He turned against your family when that plan failed. In his anger, he eventually became a traitor and joined the allies of the Enemy Way. His desire to lead the Itiwana against a foe made him a weapon those same foes could use."

Kia tilted her head. "I know about Hobomok. Why are you telling me this?"

"You should learn from your family history," Pogum told her. "Consider the possibility that our people are best served by wisdom and loyalty, not by hatred of the enemy or the need for personal glory. Your grandfather, Yana-Luha, taught me that greatness is achieved by fidelity to your ethics as well as commitment to your loved ones. If you grow greater in power but your morality withers like a dried leaf, you will ultimately lose. You may slay your enemy, but you will lose your soul."

Kia began to speak, but the words didn't come. Something about what Pogum said caused her to doubt Sula-Witsa and her decision to turn away from Molowia. Had she been mistaken in her recent actions?

No, I can't waver now, she thought. *I need to protect my family. I can't worry about ethics now.*

"I... I see," she said. "You've given me much to think about, but I still need Shula-Witsa as a teacher, and I will trust him for now. Unless you can lead me to a better teacher. Such as Manitou.

I want so much to speak to him, to learn from him. If you don't trust Shula-Witsa, let Manitou be my teacher."

Pogum shook his head, still obviously troubled. "Manitou doesn't answer my summons, Kia. He does not do my bidding. Manitou is one of the most powerful of the gods, perhaps second only to Awona'Wilona. This almighty Elder only speaks to me when he wishes to speak to me."

"But you said that after you died, you prayed to him and..."

"Yes, he answered my prayer," Pogum said. "He came to me. I didn't go to him. It's his choice when we speak. If he wishes you to be his tool in a war against the Enemy Way, he will contact you. However, I must honestly say, I don't think he will."

"But why not?" she asked.

"Because no one can be trusted with such power!"

After camping out for the night, Pahana, Hayoka, Calian, and Faw-Faw resumed their journey home. Pahana took turns riding with either Calian or Hayoka, although he rode behind Hayoka for the longest stretches, much to the chagrin of Calian.

Now that the thrill of the battle had faded, Pahana was brooding about having failed to acquire the tomahawk of Awona'Wilona. It rightfully belonged to his clan, and he knew the weapon could be a valuable tool in the ongoing war with the Enemy Way. He felt shame in having failed to win the prize.

I will return to the Bitter Root Valley someday to reclaim it, he inwardly vowed. *For my family.*

He was silent for the majority of the trip home, moping silently. Glancing upward, he became distracted by a bird swooping down toward them. The black bird landed on Gray Shadow's horns. Hayoka was about to shoo it away, but Pahana held his arm. "That's Black Crow. It belongs to my father."

"Oh, sorry. I didn't know."

"What's it doing here?" Calian asked.

"Astute question," Pahana said. "I would surmise that if Black Crow is here, my mother must have sent it. The Shakowin probably has concerns about my being away so long,"

"Your grandmother is unhappy with your absence," Calian said. "She sent me to find you."

"I thought as much," Pahana replied, dreading what Atira would say when he returned home. "Despite our failure, we still have much to do, and we can't dwell on this defeat. Come along. Let's head home."

An angry Kia was still arguing with Pogum. She continued to justify her decision to take on Shula-Witsa as her new mentor, despite Pogum's insistence that the fiery Sky Elder had an agenda that made him untrustworthy. Kia would not be dissuaded from her goal to have a teacher who could allow her to develop into the ultimate mystic champion of the Sky Elders.

"You, above all, should appreciate my need for more power," Kia said. "You've seen how dangerous the enemy is. They killed you!"

Pogum leaned on his spear as he scanned the area for more beasts. "I understand your desire. Just be careful, young one. Power is not as easy to control as you may think it is. You might indeed find yourself becoming more powerful, but you may also find yourself becoming less compassionate and less human. Just remember, it's the strength of the heart that matters, not the strength of muscles or the level of magical power. If your teacher instructs you in attaining power but not in loyalty, morality, or devotion, he is not a worthy teacher."

Kia began pacing, frustrated at Pogum's resistance regarding her efforts to increase her power. "I will consider your words, as we are family. But for now, I would continue to get stronger because that's what I need to do. So please, tell me how I can find Manitou or Kokopelli or some other teacher within this realm who can help me increase my strength."

"I ask you once more to think carefully," Pogum said. "Please take some time to reflect. Talk to Molowia. At least talk to your mother or your grandmother."

Kia was on the verge of losing her temper, but controlled herself and tried a different tactic. "Think on this, Pogum. If someone can teach me more about my abilities, I can learn to use them wisely. I can be smarter if I can better understand what I'm becoming."

Pogum considered this latest argument. "Wisely, eh? It's good to hear that word coming from your lips. Learning to use your power wisely is the best thing you've said since you arrived here. Yes, I think someone should teach you about using your power wisely."

"So you agree?"

"I agree that you should be taught wisdom," Pogum replied. "When I faced the Wendigo, I knew that only intelligence would allow me to overcome such a mighty foe. I had to use my mind, just as your father always did. He was a cunning one, I recall."

"He is," Kia said in admiration of her father.

"Indeed, so," Pogum said. "The way he out-witted the Vykans was a wonderful sight to see. And in the time that I've been here, I've realized that it's not just about overpowering your foes. It is also a matter of out-thinking them. I've had many seasons here in this realm to think about using my own skills more cleverly in order to defeat the strangest foes imaginable. I can accomplish more by finding ways to deter them before they even begin. Remember, Kia, the greatest thing you'll ever learn is that there's much more to fighting than just being powerful."

"But will you help me?" she snapped impatiently.

"Yes, Kia, I will help you," Pogum said. "I will teach you, because I'm glad you're taking this route. I wouldn't want to see you corrupted by power without wisdom."

"Good," she said, relieved. "Where can we go? What can you show me? Who will introduce me to the secrets of the unknown?"

Picking up his shield, he gestured for her to follow him. "Come with me, young Kia. There are so many things in this realm you should see and so much you can learn."

"I will follow where you lead," she said, satisfied that she had persuaded him.

He walked briskly, and she had trouble keeping pace with him. As they traversed the alien world, Kia saw bizarre sights for which there were no words. Astonishing vistas, perplexing shapes, and enigmatic creatures overwhelmed her young mind. Peculiar sounds and unfamiliar colors filled her senses. Foreign smells assailed her but also seduced her. There were so many things she could never hope to describe to anyone without the proper frame of reference.

This curious domain was almost incomprehensible. *Magnificent! This world is so different. So unusual. So beguiling. I never imagined what I was missing. What miracles can I learn here that I can take with me back to the real world? What mysteries can I uncover that will help me defeat the Enemy Way? What can I use to make me the most powerful shaman ever?*

Pogum pointed out unfathomable oddities on their trek through this cryptic world. He showed her creatures whose wail of mourning caused dismal despair. Others had voices that were serene and calming, singing songs of such irresistible peacefulness and beauty that they inspired the listener to want to give up the battle and surrender. She saw other creatures who did nothing but fight, even against their own kind, because all they wanted to do was destroy and kill and see blood. She also saw ogres who sat waiting for something without ever acting. The ogres sat in groups, whispering to each other but not really listening, because they didn't have any interest in anything. She saw flames that burned through solid rock. She saw ice that would not melt in the heat. She saw insects that glowed like tiny suns. Myriad things that no mortal had ever seen before assailed her mind, and she marveled at all of it.

And then she saw the demonic flying head.

CHAPTER TWENTY

Pinga sat meditating on the steep ledge outside her rock-hollow home chamber, situated among the cliff housing. Despite her faded powers, she used the dregs of her divine abilities to see if she could summon up a vision revealing where her son was. She knew Tawa was beyond the reach of her diminished power, but she hoped Pahana was close enough that she could feel her son's presence.

After an hour of trying, she opened her eyes and looked sadly at the horizon. *This One senses nothing. Either her powers are too weak, or my son no longer exists. She prays that the flaw is in herself.*

She stood, turning to retreat into her chamber, when she heard Aholi's voice shouting in the distance. At first, she couldn't understand what he was saying. She cupped a hand to her ear and finally understood the faint words she was hearing.

"He has returned!" Aholi shouted. "Pahana is back."

Pinga sighed with relief. *Thank the Elders.*

In the distance, she saw the two bison, the three riders, the giant, and the wolf all crossing the green fields of the Land of Everlasting Summer, approaching the Deep Well. She didn't even care if he had succeeded in the mission that Manabazo had arranged for the Mudheads to send him on. She was just glad to see him safe and well.

As the bison trod through a mud hole, the riders spotted a pig sitting calmly in the sludge, seemingly unconcerned about the large animals stomping past him, and the wolf that accompanied them. Pahana found the pig's calmness strange.

"Pahana has returned," the pig said. "Did you bring with you a weapon you've earned?"

"Oh, Manabazo," Pahana said without enthusiasm, having hoped he would not run into the Elder so soon. He wasn't ready to discuss the incident yet. "What are you doing in the mud?"

"A premonition, my friend. This is how I envisioned your task would end," Manabazo said. "I see no weapon in your grip, young lad. This makes me very sad."

Calian reminded silent, embarrassed. Hayoka was still not used to this shape-shifting being, who looked like an animal and spoke in such a strange way. *Shipapa-Lina continues to baffle me.*

"I admit my failure," Pahana said, hiding his humiliation. "But this is merely a temporary circumstance. I will have that weapon, I vow."

As the bison rode onward, Manabazo lagged behind in the bog. "You do believe so, I can tell. But this failure does not bode well."

It was the strangest creature in this strange land. At the top of a bluish-gray hill, peaking out of the mist, lurked Kanon-Sistonti, a giant, demonic head. The bodiless being was a bull-sized demon, possessing fiery-red eyes, gator-like fangs, and a tangle of long, matted gray hair. The head floated above the ground, staring coldly at them as they approached. Kia gasped, terrified at the sight of it.

"This is what I wanted to show you," Pogum said, pointing to the flying head. "This creature is the only one I have not been able to defeat. This carnivorous monstrosity is clearly the most dangerous demon in this realm of deadly menaces. And the smartest."

"It's horrible!" she said fearfully. "Will it attack us?"

"No, not yet," Pogum answered, glaring at the head with controlled rage. "This creature is not yet interested in crossing the veil of realms, although he may soon change his mind. He is waiting."

"For what?" she asked.

"For more knowledge," Pogum replied. "The demon is observing and learning."

"What is he learning?"

"Too much," Pogum answered. "And it troubles me. He is observing me, above all. He's also listening to what lurks beyond the veil, just as you heard my voice. He wants to know what the defenders of the Tree of Life will do. He's listening to Tawa and the Itiwana and others who defend Yaxche. He is listening to learn how they react and what their weaknesses are. He is always studying. He's a patient creature."

"Is he powerful? Kia asked.

"All smart creatures are powerful, Kia," he answered. "It's what they choose to do with that power that makes them dangerous."

"And what do you think he will do with it?" she asked.

"This creature wishes to find a way to free Malsumis, of course," Pogum replied. "Isn't that the goal of all among the Enemy Way? When they unleash Malsumis, the simmering war which has already begun will explode like a volcano. What we have seen so far will be like children scuffling, compared to the chaos when Awona'Wilona battles Malsumis once again."

Kia knew the defeat of Awona'Wilona would bring an eternal winter upon Ulah-Nane, and possibly for places far across the Great Water. "How will the creature do that? How will he free Malsumis?"

"I don't think his plan is fully formed yet," Pogum said. "He's still watching and listening and learning and planning. But when he is satisfied he has sufficient information, he will attempt to defeat me. And if he does, he will pierce the veil and cross into Ulah-Nane. Whatever dread plan he has concocted, he will enact. And if he succeeds, then Malsumis will rise from his volcano and the war will begin in earnest. We're the only hope to stop it."

Dagwona watched from her covert vantage point as the three young men and Faw-Faw returned to the safety of their home. She grimaced with bitter disappointment at the sight of Pahana returning unharmed, despite multiple attempts to destroy him. Her hatred of Tawa burned inside her, stirring a vindictive urge to kill his son.

But she did not attack. She watched Hayoka riding on the same bison as Pahana. She knew that if she attacked now, Hayoka might be injured. There was something about Hayoka that the witch liked. And even if she hadn't been so physically attracted to him, she felt he might be a useful tool in her war against Tawa and his tribe. Therefore, she slipped away, sparing Pahana's life. She could not rid herself of the anger she felt, knowing that both Tawa and his son still walked Ulah-Nane. Needing someone to grouse to, the witch tracked down her sometimes ally Agwara the Snow Fox

Spirit. Agwara was still lurking near the lake where Ti-Typhion dwelled.

"Pahana perseveres!" Dagwona shouted in anger, her voice echoing in the forest. "Pathetic Puk-Wudgies! Foolish failures."

Dagwona ranted to Agwara, furious that Ti-Typhion, and the Puk-Wudjies, had failed to destroy one man. Agwara only half-listened to her babbling complaints, all the while thinking ahead to their next move.

"Silver skinned swine still survives," Dagwona yelled. "Shipapa-Lina scum sits safely. He's home."

"Indeed, survived he has," the snow fox spirit said, moving in a slow circle around a tree. "Home has Pahana and his companions safely reached. Formidable friends, the man has. If destroy him we will, then lure him from his allies we must. Alone, he must be. Proper bait we must find."

"Ah, alone," Dagwona said. "Luring little leader. Intriguing idea."

Agwara sat down. "How to bait the son of Tawa away from his people, we must decide. What could cause the temporary ruler to leave his tribe, I wonder? Hmmmm."

"Speak some schemes," Dagwona said impatiently.

Scratching his ear, Agwara considered possible plots. After a few moments of silence, he had a glimmer of an idea. "What do Itiwana fight to protect, eh? The Tree of Life, it is. Lure him away by threatening the tree Yaxche, we will."

"Splendid suggestion," the witch said.

Agwara displayed his row of sharp teeth, smiling smugly. "An idea I have. Come with me."

"What can we do to stop him?" Kia asked, still frightened by the sight of the floating head, which gazed at her with sinister intent.

"We must first learn what his plans are," Pogum replied, facing the head, with his spear and shield at the ready. "You can help me with that."

"How?" she asked. "What can I do?"

"You are a shaman, are you not?" Pogum asked.

"Yes," she said, with pronounced haughtiness. "I'm a very powerful shaman. Perhaps the most powerful in all of Ulah-Nane."

"Certainly not the most humble," Pogum replied with a sardonic chuckle. "But if you are indeed so powerful a shaman, you have the ability to look into the minds of others, do you not?"

Kia knew many shamans could perform this feat, but she had not mastered the ability yet. However, she did not want to tell Pogum that fact. She was embarrassed to admit her limits to the legendary Pogum.

"Yes, of course I can," Kia said, trying to sound confident. "I've done it many times."

"Good," Pogum said, gesturing to the hill. "Then I ask you to look into the mind of this ugly creature to find out what he's learned and what diabolical ideas he may be hatching. Discover what his weaknesses are. When you ascertain this, we will find a way to stop him before he begins. And he may possibly hold the very knowledge you seek. His mind may reveal the secrets to making you more powerful."

Kia was frightened of the demonic head. She stared up the hill, wary of contacting the mind of such a horror, but she could not give in to her fear now. However terrifying she found this demon to be, she had to invade its thoughts and steal its knowledge.

"Uh, yes. Fine idea," she said apprehensively. "I… I'll begin at once."

"But be cautious," Pogum said. "The mind of a ghastly creature such as this ancient horror can be very frightening. Its thoughts will be very powerful. Be very sure of yourself before you attempt this."

"I can do it," she cried with false confidence.

Closing her eyes, she outstretched her arms, pointing her fingers at the carnivorous head. Kia fully unleashed her shamanic power, letting it pour completely out of her, utterly unrestrained. Unbridled, numinous power assailed the flying head.

The demon head was unimaginably old and dreadfully intelligent. It fixed its infernal eyes on Kia, clearly aware she was trying to read its mind. Squinting hatefully, the creature utilized it's his own formidable mental defenses.

Kia screamed in psychic pain, knocked rearward by the backlash. She staggered backward several feet, barely keeping her balance. Kia clutched your head, staggered by the assault.

"What did he do to me?" she cried, aghast. "It hurts so much!"

"Stay calm, Kia," Pogum said, putting his hands gently on her shoulders. "Look at me. Breathe deep. The pain will pass. I know. I've seen others try."

"I've never felt such horrible power," she said meekly.

"I told you this would not be simple," Pogum said. "He's an eternal creature. This is just an example of what you'll have to deal with if you wish to fight the Enemy Way, Kia. Consider that."

Kia realized he was trying to dissuade her. This angered her, and she refused to be defeated. "Let me try once again."

"I would not advise it," Pogum said. "If you must, be careful."

Kia summoned her waning courage and focused her thoughts once again. More determined than before, she allowed her power to burst free with furious fervor. She battered at mental barriers, fighting to break through the defenses of the strange, ancient mind. Once more, she faced formidable resistance. His dark, inscrutable, arcane thoughts were beyond terrifying. She saw visions of inhuman tortures no mortal was meant to see.

Kia screamed once more, agonized and horror-struck. She recoiled and broke contact with the enemy. Staggering, she tripped and fell onto the odd ectoplasmic soil.

"Elders, help me!" she wailed, clutching her head. "The things I see in that creature's mind. I've never imagined any such things could exist. Those things should not exist! What I've seen is an abomination."

"The creature dreams of otherworldly horrors. It's true," Pogum said sympathetically. "Sadly, much of what you will face in this war is the same. They are nightmares come to life. These creatures will not be easily defeated. Do you wish to try again?"

"I... I'm not sure," she stammered. "I don't think..."

"No need to explain," Pogum said. "You did your best. Learn from the experience. Another attempt could do much harm to your own mind. Stop now."

Kia wanted to run away, but something stopped her. She just could not give up. Not yet. Not when the answers were so close. *I must do this!*

"I must try once more," she said, and stood up, brushing herself off.

"Don't try it, please," Pogum said.

Kia was not listening. Rage began filling her mind. *I will not let him do this to me!*

Once more, she boldly faced the horrid head. It glowered and growled in warning. The demon seemed to be sizing her up as an enemy. Its expression challenged her to try again.

Desperate and obsessed, she repeated her attack. Her unique power exploded from her inner being, bursting out with full intensity. The primordial essence of her mystical, kachina-demigoddess energy struck unmercifully at the demon. She barraged her foe with every ounce of will and power she could muster.

For a brief moment, she felt she was winning. Excitedly, she dug her way deeper into the alien mind of the demon head. The creature's psychic defenses were crumbling. She was becoming confident she would succeed.

However, its indecipherable ancient thoughts struck back with renewed force, inflicting immense, extrasensory agony in her young brain. The anguish was inexpressible, and she screamed for a third time. She had to stop, if only to keep her sanity. Kia dropped to her knees, sobbing.

"He's too much for me!" she wept. "Too powerful! I can't take any more! It's torture!"

Pogum gently put his arm across her trembling shoulders. "Cease now, Kia. You've tried your best and your courage does you credit, but the battle is over."

In the Cliff Palace of Shipapa-Lina, Pahana was addressing the Shakowin, explaining how he survived the many perils of the past few days. Sitting on the floor, facing the council, he told his strange tale. Pahana focused on his triumphs, emphasizing his bravery to make his failure in recovering the weapon seem less embarrassing. Atira, Pinga, T-Soona, and Manabazo made up his unimpressed audience. They sat in a semi-circle, facing him.

"You shouldn't have left Shipapa-Lina at all," Atira said sternly. "I advised you not to go. You left your people for days at a vital time."

"And returned with nothing to show for it," T'Soona added, never one to speak gently.

Pahana was ready with an answer to that. "It was Manabazo who sent the Mudheads to me. They told me about the weapon."

"You could have gone after that weapon on a later occasion," Atira argued. "You should have waited until your father returned. At the very least, you could have told me you would be away for days, so I could have been prepared. You promised to be back by afternoon."

Pahana attempted to change the subject. "But it seems I was correct about our new friend Hayoka. He was a great help and did not let me down. You have all been too hard on him."

"Perhaps," Atira said. "If we are wrong, we will humbly and respectfully apologize to the boy. But for now, we remain obdurate. You need more than this to convince us that the son of Hobomok is here as our friend."

Pahana's face sunk, as if he had been slapped. "You still doubt my judgment? How will I ever be a leader if you continue to treat me as a naïve child?"

Pinga leaned forward; her white eyes narrowed. "You are not the kik-mongwi yet, my disrespectful son. Your father rules here. You are a steward of the tribe. Despite being the son of Tawa, we do not owe you our allegiance. You must earn it, and you are off to a poor beginning. We will respect you when you have earned our respect."

"Your mother speaks for us all," T'Soona said, with atypical sternness.

"Listen to your mother," Manabazo advised. "She gives advice like no other."

Pinga remained silent, wanting to support her son but knowing it would be bad form to divide the Shakowin. *This One hopes Tawa returns soon to restore order and unity.*

"We are in agreement," Atira said. "You are not the kik-mongwi and you have not impressed us."

Pahana defiantly raised his tone. "Are you saying you find me ... disappointing?"

Atira locked eyes with him. "Must you hear the words before you understand? Hear them, then. We are disappointed. Be better than yourself, Pahana. Do not continue to disappoint us."

The angered Pahana slowly rose, attempting to hide his resentment. "Very well. If I can say nothing to change your mind, I relieve you of my disappointing presence. I have much to do. Excuse me."

Pahana walked out without waiting for permission to leave. The members of the Shakowin sat silently, looking at each other in disappointment. Finally, T'Soona broke the awkward quiet.

"Are you sure he's really Tawa's son?" the healer quipped.

Pinga didn't see the humor in that. "This One would know who his father is."

"I was being humorous," T'Soona said. "But what do we do about the boy?"

Atira stood up. "I may have to replace him as leader. I would hate to do it, but by the blood of Awona'Wilona, I swear I will if he errs again."

CHAPTER TWENTY-ONE

The image of Pogum looked out over the valley where he had so often hunted. The tribute to the fallen hero graced the rock face under the Mesa. Made from clay, vegetable juice, and rock powder, the drawing depicted the noble face of the revered archer, fisherman, hunter, and warrior.

Calian sat on a stone, staring at the image of the father he never knew. He had been raised on the many stories of Pogum's heroism and der-ring-do. There was not a man or woman among the Itiwana who did not regard him as a legend. Over the past 20 years, his reputation had grown to iconic proportions.

Looking up at the large drawing, Calian wished he had his own personal stories to tell about his father, but Pogum had fallen in battle before he was born. Calian had heard the tale of how Pogum sacrificed himself to destroy the Wendigo so many times he had lost count. Everyone told it in a different way. He preferred Tawa's version of the story, since Tawa had actually been there to see it, and had avenged Pogum by slaying his killer, the Berserker.

Calian heard someone treading on the grass. He turned to see his mother, Bluebird the Corn Woman, coming closer. She brought him some fruit, handing it to him with a loving smile. She looked up longingly at the image of her lost husband.

"I knew you'd be here," she said. "When I heard things went badly, I expected you to come here."

"I wish I had his greatness," Calian said in a melancholy tone as he studied the portrait.

She put a hand on his shoulder. "You do. Everyone in Shipapa-Lina speaks of you with respect. We all see much of your father in you."

"I wish I did," Calian answered. "If he were here, he would have secured the weapon success-fully. My father would have made sure Pahana succeeded. I failed."

"Stop chastising yourself, son," she told him. "No one worships the memory of Pogum more than I do, but you should never consider your-self unworthy. You have too much of your father in you to be anything less than great. Trust me, Calian. You have greatness in you, and the Itiwana are better for your presence. You'll be the hero your father was."

Kia had never felt worse. She had fallen to her knees in painful defeat. Pogum gave the teary-eyed Kia a few minutes to recover before he spoke again. He spoke gently but convincingly, hoping to get his point across.

"When you return to your own realm, you must remember what you learned here," he said. "Remember what you're fighting against. Remember their terrible power. Your confidence in fighting and conquering the Enemy Way using the shamanic powers you possess is unwise. You may win some battles, but if you attack unknown beings such as the head, you'll find your power will not be enough. There are frighteningly deadly creatures like this one, and much worse, to come. That is what you have to contend with. You'll find that your power is not sufficient to battle them in the method that you have planned. Attacking in anger is not going to work. This is not the way to defeat our enemy."

"But I must!" she shouted. "My mystic skill is all I have to offer. I have power that no one else in the Land of Everlasting Summer has ever had. I must use it!"

"And so you should," Pogum said. "But not as a ram rushing headlong into an opponent. You must act in conjunction with other older, wiser minds. Don't turn to Shula-Witsa for guidance. Seek out those you can trust to advise you properly. Trust Tawa and Molowia and Pinga. Talk to Manabazo. Let them advise you about how best to use the vast power you have. Trust your people. They are your strength."

Kia was wavering. She doubted herself. Was Pogum correct? Would she fail if she fought on her own? Did she need Molowia and the others?

"Be wise, sweet child," Pogum said. "Being strong is a benefit, but more importantly, you need to be a part of the tribe. Fighting alone is folly. I didn't fight the Wendigo alone. Don't let Shula-Witsa create a rift between you and the Itiwana. You are part of the Itiwana. Not separate from them. Remember that."

Kia sat on the mucky ground, hugging her shoulders. *I'm so close to becoming the most powerful shaman ever. I thought Shula-Witsa would be my best teacher. Do I stop now?*

"Let us get some distance from this beast," Pogum said, walking away from the hill. "Even I feel uneasy in its vile presence."

Kia lagged behind, despondent at her failure. Pogum strode ahead, vanishing into the misty terrain. Kia rose and offered a hostile side-glance to the demonic head. She looked the creature in the eye, showing that she was unbroken, even though she was retreating.

It was a mistake. Once alone with the creature, it locked its eyes on her. Kia froze when the carnivorous head stared into her soul.

"By Awona'Wilona! What...?" Kia yelled, taken by surprise. *What's happening to me?*

Kia found herself turning to the hill, utterly against her wishes. Her body was acting of its own accord. She started to walk in a straight line toward the head. *What's it doing to me?*

The carnivorous head snarled, saliva dripping from its fangs, waiting for its victim to step into its flesh-eating maw. And that victim would be Kia. It was somehow drawing her inexorably to its jaws, and she was helpless to stop herself.

Can't ... resist, she thought in a panic as the head summoned her closer. *That awful thing can probably strip a stag bare in less than a minute! If I step into its maw, I'll die horribly!*

She was horrified at her inability to stop herself. Her legs kept moving, regardless of her attempts to control them. Terror gripped her as she was faced with the fact she was walking into a savage death trap and couldn't stop herself.

She had no choice but to call for help and to hope Pogum was near enough to save her. To her alarm, she couldn't yell. The sound barely emanated from her throat, coming out as little more than a soft moan. Her slim lips would not open. There was no way Pogum could hear her. She panicked, having absolutely no way to save herself. She was completely under the head's control.

The carnivorous head commanded Kia to come closer to it, and Kia's body obeyed, despite her efforts. As frantically as her mind prayed for salvation, her body was utterly subservient to the head's overpowering dictates. It hungered, so it ordered Kia to step into its maw and abate that hunger. Kia's compliant body responded with forced obedience.

Her mind was a whirl of terror as Kia could only stare in horror as she inexorably moved nearer and nearer to the fearsome demon which controlled her. The head would not hesitate to kill her in an abominable manner.

She inched ever closer. Thirty feet. Twenty-five feet. Twenty feet. Fifteen. Closer every second. She was completely helpless to the head's commands. Her body had been seduced by the outside influence and was forced to submit to the demon's primal demands.

No! No! It cannot end this way! Please, don't let this monster rip me apart! Someone help me!

Only a few paces separated Kia from the head, which was showing no mercy. It was not inclined to show mercy. It wanted to feed, and it sensed that Kia was a potential threat. The head could eliminate a future threat and eat at the same time. Sustenance was only moments away. It opened its large maw.

The head commanded Kia to walk the last few feet, and her body unwillingly obeyed. The carnivorous head reached out with its gray hair acting as tendrils. The serpentine-like strands of hair wrapped Kia tightly in their powerful grip. Next, the head yanked her off the ground. She got a good look at the maw of the huge demonic head. The tendrils lowered the terrified captive closer to a horrible fate. Kia couldn't break free. Powerless, she watched in fear as those fangs came closer.

A long spear grazed the demonic flying head. Kia saw that Pogum had returned, running swiftly to Kia's rescue. The spear cut a gash in the head's temple but did no lethal harm. The head merely sneered at the attacking Itiwana.

"Release her!" Pogum yelled.

Having thrown his weapon away, Pogum could only swat at the head with his shield. The head dropped Kia and grabbed Pogum around the throat with its tresses of tendrils.

Kia froze, watching the battle tremulously. *I... I must do something! I must help him.*

Kia concentrated as best she could in her fearful state. She took a deep breath and summoned her remaining power. She caused Pogum's spear to float up above the ground. With an extra effort of will, she generated flames to cover the weapon. Kia ignited the spear into a flaming projectile.

"Die!" she yelled as she willed the fiery spear to impale the head in its red eye.

The head squealed in dire pain as the spear gouged out one of the eyes which had bewitched her. The howling head released Pogum. Green ooze dripped from the missing eye, the head quickly retreated. It bellowed with hatred and pain as it withdrew swiftly into the opaque mist.

Pogum dropped onto one knee, coughing and enjoying the air. "Thank you, Kia. That was not pleasant. Not at all."

Kia stood unmoving, feeling a chill through her whole body. She felt cold after the traumatic experience. The young girl had been overpowered by an incomprehensible power and almost devoured by a demon, but ultimately, she drew blood and drove the monster away.

"I was victorious!" she said. "I defeated the demon."

Pogum could see that she was becoming intoxicated with power again. "With some help from me. We worked together. Don't get overconfident. If you had been alone, you would have died."

Young Kia clenched her fists in determination. "I've learned something today. I now know the power I'm facing. You and Molowia are correct. I am not ready to battle the Enemy Way alone. Not yet, at least. It might take me several more seasons. I'll be patient. I will take your advice to be wiser. I am not as powerful as I thought. I feel … humbled. I'll seek aid from all sources, whether it's Molowia or Shula-Witsa. But one day, it will be me who humbles our enemies."

Pogum was disappointed. "I see you are determined. Your young mind is made-up. I hope you are not making a dire mistake. But if I cannot change your mind, all I can do is hope that the lesson you learned today will be the difference between what you hope to be and what you may become. I'm satisfied, at least, to see that you are still loyal to the cause. But just remember, one day, you may be asked to choose between what Shula-Witsa wants and what the Itiwana need.

When the time comes, you will have to decide whether loyalty is more important than victory."

"I will remember," she said. "I should return to Kolhu now."

"Excellent idea," Pogum said. "Would you please pass a message to my wife and child when you get back to the mortal realm?"

"Yes, of course," Kia said.

"Please speak to Bluebird, my beloved wife," Pogum said. "Tell her that not an hour has gone by in which I have not thought about her. I miss her beyond words, and I look forward to the day we will be reunited in the Holy Hunting ground. And tell my son, Calian, that his father looks forward to meeting him one day. I'm sure he's a good man. Tell him to look after his mother and to be devoted to his people and make me proud. Please tell him that."

"I will," she said.

"Thank you," he said. "goodbye, dear Kia. Be well."

Pogum watched as Kia's new spirit body began to fade. Her mortal mind slipped away, traveling once again behind the veil, back to Ulah-Nane.

I feel Kia will be important to the war in the future, Pogum thought. *I hope she acts wisely.*

CHAPTER TWENTY-TWO

Kia found herself once again in Kolhu. She was relieved that she had returned to her original body, safe in the realm of solid, physical reality. She stretched her arms out and craned her neck.

Home! It's good to be back in my own little body.

She felt her own breath and her own heartbeat. For a few moments, her body seemed foreign to her, but she quickly readjusted to being human again. It was a relief to be away from those terrible creatures, especially that nightmarish head. Although the satisfaction of spearing it had been thrilling.

Kia felt bitter disappointment when the exhilaration of being in another realm began fading. She wished she could recreate that same stimulating delight. *The experience was thrilling. If only I could go back, but I have too much more to learn.*

Kia debated her next move. Should she talk to Molowia? She very much wanted to sleep. But there was something she needed to do first. She relit the flame in the kiva and fixed her gaze on the flickering blue fire.

"Shula-Witsa!" she yelled. "Listen to me. Please answer me."

The majestic eye of Shula-Witsa again appeared. "I am here. I've come. You called me. I came. You need me. I've arrived."

"I have much to tell you," she said.

She began explaining her experience to the Sky Elder. She told him about meeting Pogum and about the flying head who she could not destroy. She lamented that she was not powerful enough to slay one demon. She told him of her desire to alter her training and accept help from others, not to be a lone weapon for Shula-Witsa. She accepted she would need to wait until she was older before she battled the forces of Malsumis directly.

As she spoke, the unblinking eye stared at her with that same mind-altering glare she had experienced before. It again tried worming its way into her young brain, turning her once more to his way of thinking. But something was different now.

"Are you doing something to me?" she asked suspiciously. "You're making me feel strange."

Shula-Witsa paused, taken aback by her alertness. When he spoke, his voice was gentler than before. "Be at ease. Be calm. You are nervous. You are."

"I suppose so," Kia said, unconvinced. "But regarding what I was saying..."

"Wait one moment. Wait, Kia," Shula-Witsa said. "I have information. I do. About the omens. Three omens. I have answers. I have."

Kia perked up; her interest heightened. The Itiwana had long tried to discover which three omens would signal the return of Malsumis. "You know what they are? Tell me!"

Shula-Witsa allowed a tense silence to hang in the air. He had found a way to regain the advantage in their relationship. "I'll tell you. I will. But not yet. Not yet."

"Why not?" she shouted.

"You doubt me. You do," the fiery eye said. "Earn my knowledge. Earn it."

"What must I do to get the information?" she asked.

"Prove your loyalty," the Elder said. "Prove it. Be my warrior. My weapon."

Kia hesitated, unsure of what to do. She remembered Pogum's warning, but she also knew how persistently Tawa and the Itiwana had sought the answer to the three omens. If she could learn this secret, it would be the most important piece of information anyone from Kolhu or Shipapa-Lina had yet discovered. How could she pass up this chance?

"Very well, I agree," she said reluctantly. "I will hold you to your word. In return, I'll continue to be your obedient student."

"An excellent decision. Wise choice," Shula-Witsa said. "Study my teachings. Be faithful. You'll become powerful. Very powerful. You shall grow. You'll change. Accept your destiny. Accept fate."

"Yes," she said. "I will."

"That is good. That's good."

The young girl felt very fatigued. "I must rest now. Please leave me."

"I'll go now. I depart."

As the image of the eye faded, Kia scowled at the idea of being forced to continue as Shula-Witsa's underling. She was becoming convinced that Pogum was correct. The Elder was manipulative and cunning.

Stressed by the experiences of the day, Kia was tempted to sleep, but another thought struck her. *What's happening to my father and brother? I should look in on them. I may not be able to destroy demons yet, but I can still protect my family.*

A patchwork of jade, forested areas peppered the august Shining Rock Mountains. Evergreen trees stood, pointing like arrows to the realm of the Sky Elders. One particular area, known as the Tesh-kwi, was a quiet zone that few people dared venture into. There was a reason for the solitude of the area.

Clinging to the side of the tallest tree in the area was an immense, emerald poshayanki, in the form of a towering grasshopper. Larger than a moose or bison, the giant insect noiselessly surveyed its domain. Its silence ended when it detected the approach of uninvited beings; the grasshopper did not like intruders in its private kingdom.

Agwara and Dagwona arrived in Tesh-Kwi, floating in grandly. Cushioned upon the updraft winds that Dagwona had created, they drifted gently down, just outside the wooded section. Agwara gestured for Dagwona to be silent.

"The speaking, leave to me," Agwara said quietly. "Carefully, must we speak with the mighty grasshopper."

Dagwona nodded, allowing Agwara to lead the way. Agwara trotted into the woods, sniffing his way toward the goddess of this green domain. They were alarmed by the loud chirping sound that echoed throughout the area.

Angry does the grasshopper sound, Agwara thought.

The high-pitched chirps became louder as they neared the great grasshopper. The chilling sounds were either a warning or an expression of the creature's anger. A feeling of dread filled even these two deadly beings. An angry poshayanki was not to be underestimated.

As they approached the tall tree, the goliath of a grasshopper turned its head and glared down at them with emotionless eyes. Its threatening chirps became loud enough to sting the ears of the two new arrivals.

"Be at peace, I implore," Agwara said, bowing his head. "No harm do we intend."

As they waited for the grasshopper to respond, they heard a clicking sound. A shadow crossed over them. Looking up, they saw a winged moth-woman hovering above them. She had human legs but no arms. Her antennae scanned them with mystic senses. With insect-like eyes, she studied them.

"Nunusa," Agwara said. "The insect kachina, she is. The tiniest winged creatures, she rules."

The hovering Nunusa responded with a longer, higher-pitched buzz. Dagwona tensed for a fight as the insect-woman buzzed menacingly. Agwara slapped her with his tail to indicate that she should remain calm. The shrewd Agwara had deduced the meaning of the enigmatic sound.

"No need for aggression, I promise," Agwara said. "Friends, we are. To help you, I came."

The wary Nunusa dropped to the ground, curious about the snow fox's offer. The great grasshopper had reduced the volume of his screeching chirps, allowing Nunusa to deal with these strangers.

Agwara knew something about Nunusa that Dagwona was unaware of. There was a long, antagonistic feud between Nunusa, the insect queen, and the ancient Spider-Mother. The two mighty queens had battled in the past. Spider-Mother had generally had the advantage but had never completely defeated Nunusa.

"A weakness in your enemy, I have learned," Agwara answered. "The Spider-Mother you can finally destroy."

Nunusa buzzed in excited anticipation at the information. She clearly wanted to know more. Agwara paused to keep her in suspense and revealed the secret she coveted. "To Ulah-Nane did the Spider-Mother once send her human disciple and avatar, the mortal Morning Star. To bond herself with this land, she did so."

Agwara explained to Nunusa that once the Spider-Mother abandoned her home in the clouds, she needed to bond herself to the land. She used Morning Star as a conduit to connect her with the plains of Ulah-Nane. When Morning Star helped plant the Tree of Life, it ensured that the Land of Everlasting Summer would always be a source of vitality and strength for her. If the tree were to die, the Spider-Mother would be weakened. However, Nunusa was a winter moth, and easily adapted to the cold weather. If the long summer ended, Nunusa might be able to slay the Spider-Mother.

Nunusa buzzed with pensive reluctance. Agwara guessed about the cause of her hesitation. "Concerned you are about the defenders of Yaxche, I assume. Fear not. Away has Tawa gone. As for his son, soon will Dagwona and I deal with him. And do not fear Manabazo, I tell you.

Directly attack you, he will not do. Vulnerable is the Tree of Life right now. Destroy it we can, and the Spider-Woman shall die! When free is Malsumis, grateful to you shall he be."

Nunusa's wings fluttered rapidly, and she buzzed with excitement. Hovering into the air, she flew up to meet with the grasshopper. Nunusa buzzed while the mighty grasshopper chirped in return. They seemed to be deep in conversation.

Dagwona scratched her head, apparently trying to understand the exchange. "Strange situation. Confusing conversation. Bothersome buzzing. Will we win?"

Agwara made a purring sound. "Worry, not. Confident am I. Agree to my plan, they will."

After several more minutes of unintelligible communication, the great grasshopper began to flap its massive wings, causing winds to blow through the local plants and reeds. As a result of this, chirping sounds began to echo from every direction. It sounded to Agwara like thousands of crickets surrounding them.

Moments later, Agwara found that he was correct. Innumerable insects, looking like grass-hoppers and crickets, appeared from their secret places in the forest and attended to their mighty queen.

The grasshopper took to the air, heading in the direction of Shipapa-Lina. Its obedient subjects followed along. There appeared to be millions of them. They filled the sky like a solid black cloud. It was a voracious cloud made of hungry, living creatures.

"Locusts a plague of," Agwara said in satisfaction. "Quite awesome to see, it is."

"Impressive indeed," Dagwona answered. "Perplexing plan. Witch wonders why."

"Dispel your confusion, let me," Agwara replied, beaming happily. "Special insects, they are. Anything can they eat. Everything is their food. Survive can no tree. Remaining standing, there will be nothing. Eaten, all florae will be. Devastation is inevitable."

Agwara explained to the witch that these particular insects, spawned from the mighty grasshopper, were capable of eating their way through any type of vegetation, even trees. They could easily reduce a forest to a field of holes with gnawed roots.

Dagwona nodded, smiling. "Everything eaten. Delightful destruction."

"Indeed so," Agwara replied.

Dagwona nudged Agwara. "Fox forgets. Pahana problem persists."

"Trust me, you must," the snow fox said. "Die, Pahana will."

Up in the north in Norumbega, the Vykans of Nuremgard were going about their daily business of hunting, fishing, and carpentry. The elders told the younger ones tales of the days of bold adventure. Despite their capacity for violence, life had become routine. But it wouldn't remain that way for long because something was about to stir up some trouble.

Agwara and Dagwona appeared in Vineland, carried by her winds. Agwara was there to enact the next phase of his plan. The snow fox spirit needed the Vykans for the next part of the plan. In order to get their cooperation, he had to rile them up with rage. Agwara, of course, was quite good at that. He approached the Vykans in their homeland under conditions of peace. His real intention was to set them on the warpath!

Soon, there would be fury in Vineland! The Vykans had been informed of the death of the fierce and powerful bear god, Nanook, who they worshipped. They learned from Agwara that not only had a mortal dared to slay the northern bear deity using the same weapon that had been denied to Giwakna, but the killer was also the leader of the tribe that they had fought before... the ones who killed not only Giwakna but the Berserker, as well. To add to the sin, this sacrilegious Itiwana had stolen a sacred object.

The Vykans, who had been so uncharacteristically indolent in recent years, acting as carpenters and raising families with the Hee-Heez, felt that long subdued killer instinct blistering to the surface. They instinctively raised their tools as if they were holding the swords and axes the Vykans used to wield so often and so well. The mood of the group was profusely clear... They wanted revenge!

Hunwulf was still the leader of the Vykans, but he was getting old and was currently suffering an illness. He was coughing a lot, and he felt drained of energy. Merely standing up had become a chore, and he spent most of his time in his wood cabin. He slept a lot these days, tended by his wife. His daily duties had been taken over by his sons, Magnus and Gunnar.

Both Magnus and Gunnar had been brought up on the stories of the glory days and great battles that had made the Vykans so feared around the world, before they settled down to their monotonous existence. There had been little in their lives to challenge them or bring them the kind of glory that their elders saw years ago. As young men, they longed to prove themselves and to find excitement and adventure. This was the first chance they had gotten to form a war party and go into battle. They latched onto the opportunity like barnacles on a whale.

The two young men were supported in their decision to attack by the Drengar. The title of Drengar was given to the most skilled and devoted warrior in the community. He had won almost every tournament. He was considered the successor to the Berserker.

The huge Nordic warrior had been bred and raised for nothing but battle and had never had a good war to prove his power. He had yearned for many, many summers and winters to see blood on his sword and to watch enemies fall in droves the way they once had before him. In his mono-syllabic way, he urged the two lads to march south and finish the unfinished matters between the Itiwana and the Vykans.

Agwara watched as the Vykans worked themselves into a primal frenzy, and then the fox decided he and Dagwona should slip away, lest Awona'Wilona learn of his involvement and punish him before Malsumis was freed. The fox spirit was satisfied with his day's work.

"Attack they will," he told Dagwona. "And then, a choice will Hayoka have to make. Motivated by his own kind will he be!"

For the next several days, the Vykans prepared for a new, long overdue war. They gleefully reacquainted themselves with their swords, shields, and battle axes. They sang songs of battle, past and future. It was as if time had turned backward again, and they were once again the frightening force they previously had been.

And then Hunwulf emerged from his cabin. He'd been sleeping in his wooden dwelling, but the noise and activity woke him. His wife informed him of what was happening. Hunwulf was incensed at not being consulted about the most important thing that had happened to the Vykans in so many seasons. He rose unsteadily and, with some help from his wife and a walking stick, he saw the sunlight for the first time in a week. He mustered all the authority he could gather because now, more than any time in recent years, he had to be the leader of the Vykans, as he had been in the faded past.

The Vykans didn't notice him right away, but when they did, they all stopped what they were doing. The Norsemen watched him walking with small, slow, delicate steps to the center of Vineland. He raised his large hands to indicate he had something to say, and he still held enough respect to demand quiet.

"No!" he shouted, and every person present recoiled at the idea that their ailing leader might try to stop this quest for glory. "No, we will not do this!"

The Drengar snorted with disgust and a murmur of agreement rose from the Nordic group. Magnus and Gunnar, trying to save face, rushed to get their father back into his cabin before the Drengar could start a rebellion.

"You shouldn't be up, father," Magnus said.

"I should be where I am meant to be," Hunwulf said as loudly as he could, stifling a cough. "And I am here to prevent the breaking of a vow."

"Which vow is this, father?" Gunnar asked.

"I gave my word to the sacred Asa Grace Maid, Lady Pinga!" Hunwulf croaked, his words ending in a cough. "I swore not to go to war with the Itiwana. I will not be made a liar of. My word is inviolate and will stand as long as I breathe the air of Vineland! There will be no war!"

Hunwulf coughed again, and his bride helped him back to his cabin. He had said his piece, and all he could do now was hope that the others still respected him enough to obey. He assumed, at least, that his sons would honor his word.

Magnus and Gunnar looked at each other with hesitant uncertainty. They had been so keen to go to war, but now their father had forbidden it. How could they go against his wishes? They had never disobeyed him before. They would dishonor their clan if they refused to comply with his commands.

"Fight!" the Drengar cried wildly. "We fight! We kill! We want blood!"

The tribe seemed to be split on the issue. Some wanted to ignore the ailing Hunwulf and avenge Nanook, while the rest remained devoted to their leader. A few of the Vykans wavered, torn between honor and devotion.

Magnus and Gunnar slipped off alone to discuss the matter privately. How could they resolve this without losing honor as warriors or as the sons of Hunwulf? After a long debate, they came to a decision. Magnus, the elder brother, charged Gunnar with a special task. Gunnar was eager to do it.

CHAPTER TWENTY-THREE

*D*anger is near, Manabazo thought. *A horrible threat is almost here!*

In his eagle form, Manabazo took to the skies. In the past few hours, the earthbound Elder had been overwhelmed by a sense of imminent jeopardy. His divine instincts were screaming a dire warning that doom was rapidly approaching. Whatever was coming, it was vast and extremely lethal.

What could it be? the shape-shifting elder wondered. *I search but cannot see.*

His prophetic perceptions relentlessly bellowed forewarnings in his mind. Manabazo continued his aerial reconnaissance, repeatedly circling high above Shipapa-Lina. He was increasingly worried about whatever terminal terror was approaching.

Kia shouted, troubled by what she was sensing. *What is it?*

She had been attempting a feat that should have been relatively simple for her at this point in her development. She was probing Ulah-Nane, looking in on her brother in Shipapa-Lina, as she had promised her father. When her spiritual sensations came close enough to get an impression of the village she was born in, she was struck by a portent of looming jeopardy.

The danger she sensed was so overpowering that the foreboding burst of emotion almost knocked her off her seat. She composed herself and attempted to refocus on visualizing the peril, but could not seem to center her apprehensive senses enough. She needed help.

"Please come to me, Shula-Witsa," she pleaded. "I need help."

Once again, that disquieting eye appeared and locked his gaze on young Kia. "I am here. I am."

Kia described the sense of danger she had experienced. "I must know what it is. I think my family is in danger."

"I will help," the fiery Elder said. "I can. You must focus. You must. Calm your thoughts. Calm them. Do not fear. Do not. Suppress your emotions. Suppress them. Envision the place. See it.

See the colors. All colors. Detect the scents. Smell it. Listen for sounds. Hear them."

Kia obeyed Shula-Witsa's instructions, centering herself with cold concentration. She imagined the sights, sounds, and smells. This allowed her to single-mindedly hone in on the region of her home village.

"No!" she cried, horrified.

"Awaken and arise", a voice shouted, disturbing the sleeping Hayoka.

A drowsy Hayoka opened his eyes, befuddled. He looked around the pit house he'd been permitted to reside in during his stay. Dawn's light shone in from above, illuminating the chamber. No one else was present.

"Who spoke?" Hayoka asked, slowly reaching for his knife.

"Dagwona declares," the voice said. "Witch warns."

"Dagwona?" Hayoka asked. "Where...?"

He spotted a small hole in the ground. Hayoka leaned closer and heard the sound of rushing air coming from it. A circle of wind blew dust and dirt in a spiral, forming a ring around the opening. He studied the swirl of air.

Is she speaking to me from there? Hayoka wondered.

"Run rapidly," Dagwona's voice commanded. "Danger descends. Shipapa-Lina shall suffer."

Hayoka leaped to his feet. "Is the village under attack? Am I in danger?"

"Hurry, handsome Hayoka," Dagwona's voice said. "Flee fast!"

Hayoka asked no further questions and rushed to the ladder that led to the surface. "I don't know what's happening, but thank you for the warning."

Hayoka emerged from the pit house and surveyed the area for some sort of danger. *Nothing seems to be wrong. What is she warning me about?*

He saw Pahana standing near the Speaking Mound, talking to Pinga. She was gesticulating her arms in agitation. *Perhaps they know something.*

He approached the pair, and overheard Pinga describing some vision she'd had. Whatever it was, she was clearly distressed.

"This One does not think it was merely a dream," Pinga said. "She has had premonitions before. This dream worries her."

Pahana looked around the village, examining his domain for some sign of an enemy. "And you can't determine exactly what form this danger will take?"

Before Pinga could answer, a pinkish-red mist materialized near the mother and son. Hayoka backed away. *Is this the danger Dagwona warned me of?*

Pahana jumped protectively in front of his mother, yelling, "Stay back!"

The moment of fear quickly ended when the mist formed into the transparent image of Kia.

The astral form of the young girl floated in front of them like a ghost. "Mother. Pahana."

"Kia!" Pinga sighed, relieved. "You frightened This One."

"I'm sorry, mother, but this is urgent," Kia said.

"What is amiss?" Pahana asked.

"Locusts!" she cried. "An unnatural swarm, capable of razing the Land of Everlasting Summer to the ground. They are led by a terrifying poshayanki."

"By Awona'Wilona!" Pinga gasped. "The locusts of the Shining Rock Mountains. They will devour our crops and even swallow up our fruits and berries. Nothing eatable will remain standing!"

Before Pahana could reply, an eagle swooped down and landed on the Speaking Mound.

"I came to warn you, but it seems Pinga already knew," Manabazo said. "Creatures that fly, I do espy. There is danger in the sky. I have spotted a swarm of excessive power. They will be here within the hour."

"We must quickly think up a defense for Shipapa-Lina," Pahana ordered.

"I fear Shipapa-Lina is only one part of the plan," Manabazo said. "They will destroy some-thing else, if they can."

Something else? Hayoka wondered. *What could they...?*

"Yaxche!" Pahana shouted. "They will also destroy the Tree of Life!"

CHAPTER TWENTY-THREE

"The tree must be defended, or our future will be ended," Manabazo announced.

"We must defend both!" Pinga interjected. "This One wishes Tawa was here."

"But he is not," Pahana said, taking control of the situation. "And we will make him proud by our next actions."

Masewa and O'Yewa came riding in on their mounts, pointing to the horizon. "There is something in the sky," O'Yewa said.

"We are not fortunate enough for it to merely be a rain cloud," Masewa commented.

"For once, you two are exactly on time," Pahana said. "Come! We have much to do."

The others followed Pahana as Manabazo fluttered onto his shoulder. Hayoka debated accompanying them, but decided against it. *This is not my home and these people have not accepted me yet. Dagwona seems to feel that the village is doomed. I must flee this place.*

Hayoka managed to slip unnoticed out of the village during the chaos of the next hour.

Not a tree or bush was left standing. Where a fertile forest had stood only minutes ago, now lay a barren field. The buzzing black shadow left nothing behind that would indicate there had ever been any life there, other than some exposed tree roots.

Leading the army of insects, the great grasshopper gobbled up entire shrubs and bushes all on its own. It could gnaw a thick branch off a tree in a few bites. As the branches dropped to the ground, the hungry swarm would make them disappear very quickly. They ate their way through dense woodlands faster than even a raging forest fire could.

The great grasshopper didn't know exactly where the Tree of Life was, or what it looked like, but the creature intended to leave no tree standing in the Land of Everlasting Summer.

The relentless carnage went on, moving inexorably closer to the Yaxche and Shipapa-Lina.

The Itiwana were frantically preparing for the incoming swarm. At Pahana's command, Calian, O'Yewa, Masewa, and Aholi were supervising the Two-Horn riders as they piled up shrubs and other flammable objects in a row below the mesa. Yoki of the Moon Clan was occupied by starting a large fire, which would be used to ignite the incendiary barrier.

Evaki, Bluebird, and Hani, the teacher, joined a group of women who were all carrying drums. Every drum in the village was taken to specifically chosen locations. While this was going on, Manabazo took to the skies in his eagle form, seeking a legion of avian reinforcements.

Pahana stood with Atira, Pinga, and T'Soona, observing the hectic preparations. He was pleased with how quickly and efficiently his people were performing their tasks. Feeling confident in his plan to protect Shipapa-Lina, he could now focus on his other problem.

"Mother, grandmother, I leave Shipapa-Lina in your care," he said.

"What?" Atira asked, stunned. "Where are you going at such a time?"

"To protect the Tree of Life," Pahana said. "That is the sacred trust of our people. Awona'Wilona has tasked us with the most vital duty of all. My father spent most of his life defending the tree. I will not let it fall under my watch."

"What will you do?" Pinga asked. "What is your plan?"

Pahana puffed out his chest proudly and smirked. "I have powers and determination and cunning. And the tree itself has unique defenses. I will drive any danger away."

"You will do this alone?" his mother asked.

Pahana began walking toward the bison pen. "Leave the matter to me. Just protect our people. The tree is my responsibility, just as it was my father's."

Pinga grabbed him by the wrist. "No, you must not go alone! This One will not watch you ride off to an unknown fate, just as your father has done."

Pahana gently touched his mother's arm. "I don't have any choice. This is my fate. This is my responsibility. While Tawa is away, I am obliged to stand in defense of the tree. The Shakowin has a duty to lead and protect Shipapa-Lina. It was my father who found the tree. Part of the eternal, primal energy of that tree runs through his body. This power has been passed on to me. I am part of the tree, just as Tawa is. I must be the one to defend it. You should know this, mother."

Pinga released his wrist. Her eyes were as sad as her voice when she whispered, "Then This One must let you go, just as she had to watch Tawa go. This is the way it must be. But at least take Faw-Faw with you."

"Oh, very well, mother. If it eases your mind."

"It will," Pinga said. "Now go, before This One sobs like an infant. Please be safe, my precious one."

She kissed her son on the cheek, and Atira hugged him tightly. T'Soona stood aside, giving the family a private moment.

"You're making me proud," Atira said affectionately. "I should never have..."

"Say nothing more," Pahana said. "Sometimes the words that are not spoken are the truest of all. I go, now. Guard our people well."

Pahana located Faw-Faw carrying wooden kindling. He communicated his desire for the big Wood Man to accompany him. Not fully comprehending, Faw-Faw grunted a "gug" sound indicating a willingness to serve and followed behind Pahana.

With a mixture of trepidation and excitement, Pahana leaped onto his father's old bison,

Mountain Fury. He hadn't had an opportunity to train and tame a replacement, and so he fetched the biggest bison in the land. The powerful Mountain Fury knew Pahana well because the son of Tawa had ridden on his father's steed many times. Pahana had been a small child when he first took a ride on the mighty mount. He knew this was the strongest animal in Ulah-Nane.

"I know you expected a rest, large one, but it's time for one last day of glory," Pahana said, patting the bison. "Let's ride!"

Mountain Fury galloped off, lacking the speed of youth but with a size and power no other bison could match. Pahana felt secure on the animal's back, despite its age. He knew his father wouldn't approve of dragging the loyal animal back into service, but this was an urgent situation. Faw-Faw ran alongside them with his long-legged stride.

Atira put her arm reassuringly over Pinga's shoulders as they watched Pahana ride off to possible, and even probable, death.

"He's his father's son," Atira said.

"Indeed," Pinga said. "This one has never loved her son more than at this moment."

Atira agreed. "I am anxious to tell Tawa about this when he returns."

I know I'm dying, Tawa thought.

There was no other possible way to describe the horrible weakness he felt. He knew the life was draining out of him. He had lost a considerable amount of blood, and the infection was raging through his body. The chilled winds ripped through his frail body, sapping his energy.

Pahana had been too weak to hunt for any game, and so all he'd eaten for days was some nuts and berries. And although he was finally moving into the warmer zone of the region where Yaxche warmed Shipapa-Lina, the cold had done its work on his body. He was burning with fever, and it was a fight to stay awake and conscious. He was terribly tired, but he didn't want to sleep because he feared he would not wake up again.

The words "I must reach home" kept repeating in his brain, urging him to sail on in the longship. It had been almost two days since he had slept. *Must stay awake. Must reach home.*

After an almost unendurably long voyage, he mercifully reached the point where he could disembark. He tried to walk, but his knees gave out on him. It took considerable effort to stand up at all. On shaky legs, he led Brave Fire to land. It took all the strength he could muster to climb up onto his mount.

Almost home. One more day. Perhaps two. I must reach home.

He teetered on the back of Brave Fire, trying not to fall off, although his head kept drooping and his eyes kept closing. He fought the fatigue as best he could, knowing he was so close to home, but his valiant struggle was in vain. He lost consciousness and fell off his mount, hitting his head as he tumbled to the ground. He lay there for several hours as the life force slowly faded from him. And then someone found him.

CHAPTER TWENTY-FOUR

The dark, gray mass of ravenous insects gnawed their way through the valley and approached Shipapa-Lina. The giant grasshopper itself was nowhere in sight, but its absence would not save the Itiwana and their crops. The swarm was only minutes from the village and showed no sign of stopping.

Atira stood atop the Sun Temple, looking across the valley at the merciless plague of locusts approaching. *May Awona'Wilona defend us!*

She waved her arms and sent a signal to Evaki and the women of the Bow Sisterhood. Evaki signaled back and began playing her drum. Bluebird, Hani, and the other women joined in. They beat on their drums with considerable vigor. Upon hearing this, the men of the Two-Horn Riders began to yawp an earsplitting war cry. It echoed across their section of the valley.

Enacting the next step of the plan, Aholi responded by shouting, "Bring the flame!"

In response, Calian, O'Yewa, and Masewa began lighting torches from the fire Yoki had been tending and tossed them into the barrier of kindling. The dry shrubbery ignited quickly and spread in both directions. A wall of flame rose between Shipapa-Lina and the swarm.

When the locusts neared the city, they were disturbed by the raucous noise. The insects were sensitive to sound, and the booming blare confused them. They momentarily stopped gorging themselves, wary of the clamor.

Billowing columns of smoke wafted up from the blazing barrier like a flowing gray curtain. When the locusts sensed the heat of the flame and smelled the burning shrubs, they were afraid. The swarm stalled, unwilling to come any closer.

And then the birds came. Led by Manabazo in his eagle form, the feathered, flying legion appeared. The transforming Elder enticed and attracted the other birds with his sounds and motions. Hundreds of them gathered around him, enthralled with this eldritch avian. The birds eagerly followed him back to the field near the mesa, energized by this extraordinary eagle.

When the stimulated flock of birds saw the invading swarm of locusts, they switched to predatory mode. The birds regarded the locusts as either a threat or a meal. Whichever the reason, the birds attacked. The feathered flock began gobbling up multitudes of locusts. Scores of insects were torn apart or swallowed by the aggressive, tenacious flock. The gigantic swarm was whittled down rapidly.

Terrified of the birds, the swarm forgot their hunger or the commands of the great grasshopper. Their tiny brains could hold only the thought of escape. Survival instincts taking over, the locusts retreated, fleeing from the valley, leaving Shipapa-Lina unharmed.

The gleeful Itiwana unleashed a celebratory cheer, watching the threat disappear into the distance. Their crops were safe. The joyful women began dancing, and the men sang triumphantly.

Atira waved victoriously at the rest of the Shakowin, smiling proudly. She mouthed the words "we did it" to T'Soona, who cupped his hands together and whispered, "Of course we did."

Everyone joined in on the merriment, except Pinga. She sat quietly, wondering about the fate of her husband and child. Would they return to her? Would she see her loved ones again?

Tawa lay unconscious when the three strangers found him. The three new arrivals stood over the wounded, dying form of the Itiwana chieftain. Brave Fire, the bison, who had waited protectively near Tawa all this time, snorted and reared his horns in the direction of the approaching trio.

The three men were all wearing animal pelts and cactus thorns. If Tawa had been conscious, he would have recognized the attire, which marked them as Tunerak Destroyers, adherents of the Winter Elders. They served Dagwona, the Whirlwind Witch.

"Who is this?" one of them asked, looking down at Tawa.

Brave Fire lurched forward, warning them that he was there to protect his master.

"Ho there, smelly beast," the second Tunerak said. "Behave yourself."

The third man took a good, long look at Tawa. "He's not one of us. He is probably a member of the local tribes."

"Are we hungry again?" one of them asked with a chuckle.

"He'll make a good sacrifice to Malsumis," the first man said. "Let's take him."

As they kneeled to lift him up, Brave Fire thrust his horns at the trio. The threesome backed away, wary of the animal's size. Brave Fire would not leave his master's side. The Tunerak Destroyers knew they were going to have to deal with the big beast.

The trio spread out, flanking the animal. They planned their attack. But they would not attack as men. These strangers were not simply Tunerak Destroyers. They were skinwalkers, in the service of Malsumis and the Enemy Way.

Nodding and grinning at each other, the skin-walkers transformed into their bestial forms. They howled and salivated and moved in for the kill.

Catastrophe had come to the Tree of Life. The mighty grasshopper ate his way across the landscape, with his endless army of locusts obediently trailing behind, gobbling up all existing flora. Although the giant poshayanki had no particular interest in the Tree of Life, he was unwittingly headed toward the most important location in the world.

High atop Manitou's Rise, Yaxche, the sacred tree, stood unnoticed by the world. It was ordinary and indistinctive by design. Its lush leaves blew in the wind, making a soft brushing sound. For more than 300 years, it had remained untouched by the Winter Elders, who wanted nothing more than to see it fall. Shielded from the eyes of those who would do it harm, the tree normally needed no additional protection beyond what it usually possessed. Tawa had decided that the presence of warriors guarding the tree would give away its location. Anonymity was a better defense than men with spears.

Mapingwari, the sloth, sensed the approach of danger. Although the beast was normally an indolent and passive brute, it became alarmed by what its primal senses were detecting. Roused from its usual slumber, it growled warningly.

Simultaneously, the host of protective bees that perpetually safeguarded the tree immediately flew into action, circling the tree like a living fence.

The grasshopper sniffed out the presence of Mapingwari. Detecting a possible opponent, its competitive, territorial impulses were triggered. The grasshopper altered course and charged directly for the huge sloth.

As the grasshopper came closer, Mapingwari knew his present, slow-moving form was no match for the colossal insect. With an angry snort, the sloth began to transform. The massive animal stretched to become wider and denser. Its fur vanished, and its skin became baggy, now covered with moles and warts. It began to resemble a wild boar with lethal, yellow tusks. Mapingwari had recreated itself. It had been many centuries since it had taken the form of Squonk the hideous.

The grasshopper attacked Squonk, which responded by thrusting its sharp tusks at the giant insect. The grasshopper was hurt, but did not stop trying to sink its teeth into the boar. The two titanic poshayanki locked up with savage abandon. In their mindless fury, they rolled down the hill, snarling and biting.

The locusts had followed their leader to the top of the hill. They feared Squonk and so avoided the fight, leaving the grasshopper to battle alone. They decided to make a meal out of the tree. However, they did not reckon with the killer bees who defended Yaxche. The venomous circle of bees parried, stung, and rammed any locusts that came near the tree. The attacking locusts could not reach Yaxche, although wave after wave kept trying.

A mile away, Pahana arrived atop Mountain Fury, with Faw-Faw running close at his side. They saw the plague of insects attempting to reach the tree, as well as the two monsters fighting at the foot of the hill.

I'm too late. Pahana thought. *What should I do now?*

Pahana nudged the big bison forward. "Come, Faw-Faw. We may not be gods, but we shall fight so valiantly today that the gods will notice us again."

Before his bison could trot more than a few steps, Pahana was cut off by that same pink-ish-red mist he had seen hours earlier. This time, he knew what it was even before the image of his sister materialized. Faw-Faw stared slack-jawed, utterly confused.

"Wait, Pahana!" Kia's astral form cried. "Don't rush into this peril recklessly."

"This is no time for caution," Pahana said. "It's a day for bold action. That beast may be slayable. Following that, perhaps I can use my natural-born powers to somehow drive those insects from the tree. It may not work, but I am obliged to try."

"Let me do that for you," Kia said. "I promised our father I would protect you."

Pahana's brow furrowed. "You protecting me? I am the older brother. I should be protecting you."

CHAPTER TWENTY-FOUR

"Stop being so proud, you big buffoon," Kia snapped. "Let me help."

"How?"

"Stand and behold, big brother," she said.

The transparent, hovering image of Kia put her fingers to her temples and closed her eyes. She muttered something imperceptible, chanting repetitively. For the first minute, nothing happened, and Pahana was running out of patience.

"No more of this," Pahana said. "I must..."

His voice trailed off when he saw the enormous swarm of locusts abruptly back away from the tree. Their retreat surprised Pahana. The inexplicable withdrawal was not limited to the area near the tree. The plague of locusts speedily fled, crossing the devastated fields. They continued fleeing back the way they came. Pahana watched the unexpected exodus in awe. The swarm got smaller and smaller in his vision until the vast insect legion vanished over the horizon. The sound of their buzzing dissipated.

The threat was gone.

"Miraculous!" Pahana gasped. "Sister, did you cause that?"

Kia opened her eyes, but she seemed weary. "Yes, I did. I have never controlled so large a group of pests before. It was harder than I thought it would be."

Pahana had mixed emotions. He was embarrassed at watching his sister save the tree, while he could only stand and stare. At the same time, he was glad the danger was past. Pahana was impressed by Kia's formidable power.

"You amaze me, little one," he said. "I had no idea you were capable of such an act. What has Molowia been teaching you?"

Kia remained silent for a moment. Pahana felt like she was hiding something, but now was not the time to discuss that. *She has done a great thing. I should have been the one to save the tree. I wanted to make our father proud. I wanted to prove myself to the Shakowin.*

"My head hurts now," Kia said. "I must rest. I leave the grasshopper to you. Goodbye, Pahana."

As the mist faded, Pahana said, "Goodbye and well done, sweet sister. Ah, this is a most perplexing day. But no time to ponder such things. Come, Faw-Faw. Our work is far from done."

Pahana and Faw-Faw charged to the foot of Manitou's Rise, where Squonk was still battling the grasshopper. Pahana did not recognize the current form of Mapingwari, although he had been told by Manabazo that the sloth could do such a thing in an emergency. However, he did know that the grasshopper was his enemy, so he focused his assault on the jade giant.

Squonk and the grasshopper flailed wildly at each other, tusks and mandibles colliding in animalistic rage. Neither monster was inclined to show mercy in this battle. Only the death of the other would satisfy the ultimate winner.

Pahana urged the large, powerful Mountain Fury to charge as fast as he still could; the bulky bison rammed horns first into the angry grass-hopper. The enormous insect chirped loudly, injured by horns that were meant to destroy him. All the Itiwana bison had been specially bred to fight poshayanki. Mountain Fury had once injured the avian terror Achiyala, and now the mighty mount wounded the grasshopper. Moments later, Faw-Faw lifted a small boulder and slammed it down brutally on the grasshopper's antennae.

Squonk took advantage of the situation and moved in for the kill. The boar stuck his tusks into the injury point where the bison horns had torn into the grasshopper's body. The grasshopper squealed and screeched, flopping around in pain, and then finally became limp.

An elated Pahana cheered triumphantly while Squonk, Faw-Faw, and Mountain Fury repeatedly stomped on the dying creature. After minutes of this, the grasshopper moved no more. A posh-ayanki was dead.

Pahana laughed as he looked down at the slain monster. "Marvelous. I hope the rest of you don't mind, but I'm going to take credit for this. Please don't say anything to anyone. This must be considered my kill. My father will be proud."

Squonk snorted again, slumping in exhaustion. Its appearance blurred as it transformed back into its non-threatening sloth form. It was Mapingwari, once again. The tired sloth yawned and slowly turned. In its usual, casual style, it inched its way back up the mountain.

"Goodbye, Mapingwari," Pahana said. "You are a good and loyal servant of the Sky Elders, as are you, Faw-Faw. And Mountain Fury is still the king of beasts. Well, I suppose we should..."

Pahana felt strong wind gusts forming. His hair was blown in the breeze. "Oh no. This is not a good omen, Faw-Faw."

He peered upward, expecting to see an enemy approaching. And he was correct. The battle was not yet over. Pahana felt rather giddy at the prospect of a fight. He hadn't done much to defeat the enemy thus far, but now he may find an opportunity to show his quality.

"Thank Awona'Wilona. A new adversary appears," Pahana said. "The gods are kind."

Drifting in on an air stream, the distant figures of Dagwona and Agwara could be seen approaching Manitou's Rise. Pahana laughed like an excited child. "Finally. A fight."

Pinga stood on the cliff above the rocky overhang that cast its shadow over the valley. She stared out at the vastness of the Land of Everlasting Summer, seeing the damage that the swarm had done. She hoped the forest would grow back quickly because hunting and foraging were so important to the tribe,

Pinga also pondered the fate of her husband and son. Pahana still had not returned from his mission to protect the Tree of Life, and no one had any word from Tawa in two full moon cycles. Was her family alive? Would they be coming home?

Atira joined Pinga upon the cliff. She had become very close to the pale-skinned beauty over the years.

"You've been here since the day was young," Atira said.

"This One is distraught," Pinga said. "She fears for her loved ones."

"They're my loved ones, too," Atira pointed out.

"This One did not mean to imply otherwise," Pinga responded. "She knows you must be concerned as well. This One simply feels so helpless. She had great power once, but now that power is gone, and all she can do is wait with desperate worry."

"I feel your frustration," Atira replied. "But while we wait, there is still much to do."

"Indeed, the damage to the forest will make things hard," Pinga said. "Large game will become scarce."

"There's still a large amount of undamaged forest beyond the mesa," Atira said. "The animals probably fled there to get away from the swarm. Our hunters will find them. And my flute will help draw them closer to us. As for the foraging, I have a surprise for you. Look here."

The old longhouse where the Shakowin used to meet before the cliff housing was built stood nearby. Atira led Pinga inside to show the lovely albino the contents of this special storehouse. Pinga saw many, many baskets full of nuts.

Atira beamed proudly. "T'Soona suggested this. In the event the Winter Elders ever succeed in their plan to bring endless winter upon us, he suggested we should be prepared. So, I told Hani to organize the kids into scouting expeditions and forage extra nuts. They've been doing this for several full moons now. I wanted to surprise Tawa with it."

"This One marvels at your resourcefulness," Pinga said

"I often marvel at myself."

After the tremendous effort of saving her brother, Kia's head ached, and she was utterly exhausted. She wanted to savor her success, but she was depleted of energy. *I'll rest for just an hour. Simply to relax my mind. Just a short sleep and then I'll get something to eat, but I'll look in on Pahana again soon.*

Kia lay down on her bed of hay. She had over-taxed herself commanding those locusts. Her little head was pounding. The moment her cheek touched the straw bed, she immediately fell asleep. But her sleep was not peaceful. Kia had strange nightmares. She saw visions of attacking monsters, particularly that awful head. She slept fitfully, pitching back and forth in her slumber.

Her new power, however, did not rest. That amazing, unfettered power that she possessed was still spinning in her mind, looking for a way to lash out. A sleeping mind could not contain such a storm of magical ability. Even while she dreamed, her uncanny energies were active.

She dreamed of the future. She saw unclear images, mostly of strangers. She heard sounds and words and could make nothing of them. It was a jumble of fragments of days that had not yet happened.

But one vision did become clear. She saw images of her father. She saw Tawa. She saw others mourning him. He was dead.

No! Father!

Kia was jarred awake. She sat up, heart pounding. *That cannot be real. It must be a bad dream. My father can't die!*

Kia sat shivering, biting her lips, tears in her eyes. *Is this a real vision or just a dream? Or is this just my fears taking the form of visions? I must know. I must master the ability to see the future clearly. I must know if Tawa lives or dies!*

CHAPTER TWENTY-FIVE

Carried by the buoying winds of the witch, the two mystic malefactors known as Dagwona and Agwara hovered above the field, cackling in satisfied joy, until they floated lightly to the base of the hill. The deadly duo looked at Pahana, who stood defiantly.

"He's here," Dagwona said, cackling. "Beautifully baited. Perfect plan."

Agwara howled merrily. "Near the life tree, we must be. Followed you, we did. Surely, Mapingwari, that must be. Yaxche, must be close."

"The two triumphantly traced the tree," Dagwona replied. "We win."

Pahana leaped down from the bison. "Not until you've beaten me, Witch. You are merely the wind. I am the storm!"

"The challenge, we accept," Agwara said. "Long have I waited to see you dead."

"Pathetic Pahana," the Whirlwind Witch bellowed, shaking a fist at him. "Blood begins!"

As the witch and the snow fox flanked Pahana, Faw-Faw suddenly charged Agwara. The speedy snow fox barely evaded the Wood Man's attack. It leaped several yards away, crouching defensively.

"Clumsy and slow is the Wood Man," Agwara said. "Quick and agile is Agwara. Catch me, he will not."

Pahana pointed to the snow fox. "Keep the mischievous menace occupied, Faw-Faw. I'll attend to him after I deal with this damned witch."

"Snow spirit superfluous," Dagwona said. "Not needed now."

"I need no one either," Pahana said. "Come at me!"

Dagwona raised her arms, and the winds began to increase. She attempted to use the strong winds to launch loose objects at him. Whatever was lying around could be hurled as a weapon. Before she could complete her attack, Pahana merely laughed. He casually pointed downward. Baffled, Dagwona looked at her feet, and she saw ice forming on the ground beneath her. She jumped back with an angry hiss.

"You can try to utilize your wind powers, Witch," Pahana said. "But I will stop you, just as my mother did. And I am more powerful than she is. My capabilities are more than equal to yours."

Enraged, Dagwona tried a different tactic. She balled up her fist, and static energy crackled as if her hand were a conduit for electricity. "Dagwona delivers death!"

Pahana responded by blowing his mastop-kachina breath and using his inherited northern ice powers. His breath created an icy coating around Dagwona's fist. The ice quickly turned to water, due to the heat of her lightning charge. Pahana screamed in shock and pain at the backlash of her power.

"Shall we continue our deadly game, Witch?" Pahana asked. "Or would you care to surrender and face an easy death?"

Dagwona snarled, glaring hatefully at him. She abruptly changed strategies again and reached under her robes, producing a long, serrated metal knife. "I impale Itiwana!"

She lunged at Pahana, who leaped aside and evaded her thrust. She continued slashing wildly at him while he ducked and dodged her assault. Dagwona switched tactics. She spun like a tornado, her blade hacking and chopping through everything it came near.

Pahana was barely managing to avoid her blade, so he evoked his icy power again. With nothing more than a thought, he created his own weapon. A long, silvery object began to grow in his hand. It expanded; solid, shiny, and with a sharp point, the object amazingly came into being out of nothing. Within moments, Pahana had used his semi-divine skills to create a spear made of solid ice.

Pahana surprised the Whirlwind Witch by swinging the ice spear at her, deflecting her knife. The witch stepped back, wary of the equalizing weapon. As she backpedaled, Dagwona slipped on the ice patch that Pahana had created. Losing her balance, she tumbled to the ground, dropping her metallic dagger.

Pahana saw his opening. Moving with desperate speed, he thrust his icy spear into Dagwona's abdomen. She screamed as the weapon pierced her body. As she looked down at the open wound in her body, her eyes widened in disbelief.

"N... no. No!"

The Whirlwind Witch slumped unmoving to the ground. Her bloodied body collapsed into the dust and dirt. Pahana could have finished her off at that moment, but chose to turn his attention to Agwara.

The swift snow fox was still evading the plodding, ponderous Faw-Faw. Agwara was much too fast for either the Wood Man or the old bison Mountain Fury. The snow fox spirit was acting almost playfully in his evasions—until he saw Pahana approaching.

With the witch's metal knife in one hand and an ice spear in the other, Pahana rushed to assist Faw-Faw and the aged bison. Agwara leaped farther away, trying to create distance between himself and his two opponents.

"You aren't laughing now, you cowardly pest," Pahana said. "I have two strong hands and a weapon for each. Do you still accept my challenge? You wanted me dead. Come and try to make your wish come true."

Agwara backed away. "No rush is there, to destroy Pahana. Much time, do I have. Wait I will, until the odds are in my favor. Fare-you-well, Itiwana. In the future, we will meet."

The speedy snow fox raced away with amazing speed, laughing. Pahana could only watch him go, knowing that the elderly, exhausted bison could never catch up to Agwara.

"One day, coward, it's I who will be laughing over your body."

Pahana looked at the destruction all around him. Nature would soon replenish the damage the locusts had done to the forest, and appropriately, small insects would eat the corpse of the great grasshopper. As for the witch Dagwona, Pahana seriously considered cutting her throat with her own knife. However, he could not bring himself to attack a wounded, dying woman—not even Dagwona.

"I leave you to think about the wasted idiocy of your wasted life," Pahana told her. "You will die alone and unmourned, knowing you wasted years of your miserable life in a failed revenge plot. I hope you die slowly, Witch. Let your final thoughts be that the Itiwana still survive. Die poorly."

The witch tried to say something in retort, but the words were muted by the blood spurting up in her throat. Pahana turned his back on her as if she were insignificant. It was his final insult to her.

"Come along, Faw-Faw. Come, Mountain Fury," he said. "Let us ride to see what's happening in Shipapa-Lina. Hopefully, my plan worked, and we can all have a rest. Let's head home."

Having smelled death so many times over so many centuries, Naya-Nazgani knew he had failed to stop the slaughter. Before he actually saw the slain bodies, the scent of blood and the ominous silence told him the gruesome story. When he stepped out of the jade foliage, Naya-Nazgani found what he feared he'd find. He found the aftermath of a massacre!

The mutilated bodies scattered around the glade had been ruthlessly torn apart by teeth and claws. Naya-Nazgani examined the bodies and found that they were still warm. The blood had not dried yet. The despicable creatures that performed this horrid butchery were still close at hand.

Seething with wrath, Naya-Nazgani reflexively tightened his grip on his intimidating ax, vowing to avenge this horrific bloodbath. *They will not escape my justice!*

An expert tracker, Naya-Nazgani, was easily capable of following the beasts who did this. There were three of them, all heading north. Naya-Nazgani followed the tracks. He began to move faster, with increased urgency. He leaped over a fallen tree, his long brown hair blowing wildly in the wind.

Naya-Nazgani was a tall, powerfully built man with old eyes. He had the stubbly beginnings of a beard over his square jaw. His head and shoulders were adorned with a brown, hooded cloak made of animal pelts. Bare-chested in the cool climate, he was unbothered by the weather. He rarely got tired, which he attributed to his zeal and determination.

He observed that the footprints slowly changed over a distance. Beginning as the clawed, animalistic tracks of the monsters he had been hunting, they morphed into normal, human footsteps. *They've resumed their human form.*

Naya-Nazgani had tracked the killers from the Big Sand to Norumbega, having been recruited for this battle because no other man could fight these enemies hand-to-hand and expect to survive. Naya-Nazgani was the world's most experienced and formidable monster slayer, having lived a very violent life.

Naya-Nazgani was a mastop-kachina and had once had a family. He was the child of Yalkai-Estsan, a kachina known as the White-Shell Woman, who chose to wed a mortal man. She had a brother named Toba-Zaschina, the Born-From-Water boy, who had a lover named Whisper. She was an innocent woman of the Wind People. That was before the monsters came.

Naya-Nazgani's mother was slain by the fierce Tracking Bear and his father by a man-eating bird. His uncle was murdered by the Rolling Stone beast, and Whisper was slain by the Great Antelope.

Emotionally crushed by these tragedies, he was planning to commit suicide until he was found by the enigmatic Red Horn, a shaman and warrior with the blood of the Uwanami spirits who live on the shore of the Big Water. Red Horn had three faces and a small horn on his forehead. Taking pity on Naya-Nazgani, Red Horn trained him to be a monster hunter. Naya-Nazgani used his training to hunt down the four creatures who had ruined his life.

After the death of his family, he still had a strong moral code and a stronger blood lust. He felt honor-bound to use his wondrous abilities to protect people from monsters. The Wind People, whose voices could travel miles on the wind, would often contact him to let him know when a monster was on the rampage and needed killing. Naya-Nazgani had spent the past century hunting killer beasts.

The Wind People had informed Naya-Nazgani about the activities of the skinwalkers, the former Antejini servants of the Salt Witch who now attacked people to sacrifice them to Malsumis. He did not know who they were serving now, but this mysterious master had performed the proper ritual to transform Antejini men into monstrosities. When Naya-Nazgani heard about this, he knew he had to be the one to stop them. No one else could.

Naya-Nazgani came across several more slain warrior braves who had fared no better against these inhuman monsters than others had. Naya-Nazgani had no time to mourn or bury the dead. He had to find the skinwalkers quickly, before more blood was spilled. From what he could deduce, the beast-men were on their way to bring the survivors as sacrifices to Malsumis. Whoever their new master was would perform the ceremony, which would not only appease the Winter Elders, it would also increase the power of the skinwalkers. *No more! Not while I breathe!*

CHAPTER TWENTY-SIX

Molowia had been keeping herself occupied with basic issues regarding the ruling of Kolhu. Like her nephew Tawa, her people were her priority.

It had been some time since she had looked in to see what Kia was doing. Given the girl's recent rebelliousness, Molowia had decided to let Kia be alone for a few days. Perhaps having some time to reflect on her unwise actions would make her more agreeable when Molowia visited her again.

I've never encountered anyone her age who was so determined, Molowia thought. *Kia is truly exceptional. Perhaps I need to find another way to reason with her. I should visit her. I must hold her dearer than I realized because I can't find it in my heart to stay angry.*

When she had the opportunity, Molowia walked to the kiva where young Kia could usually be found. She knew the girl dutifully studied her craft there day and night.

Perhaps she studies too much.

As expected, Kia was sitting in front of the fire, meditating. Her eyes were tightly closed and she seemed so deep in thought; she didn't register Molowia's arrival. Molowia felt badly about the schism in their relationship. She did not like scolding Kia or punishing her. She had missed the remarkable young girl's company over the past few days. But Kia had to learn that loyalty and honesty were very important. Until Kia learned to be honest about the use of her power, the punishment would have to remain in effect. Molowia watched the girl with satisfaction.

"Hello, Cacique," Kia replied, eyes still closed.

"Hello, Kia," Molowia replied, a bit surprised.

Molowia noted that this was something she herself often did. It was a power play to intimidate others who came to see her. *The girl is learning, but is she learning the wrong things?*

"I wish to talk to you," Molowia said, sitting down cross-legged. "I want you to understand why I've punished you. I want us to understand each other. I don't enjoy doing this, but it was necessary."

Molowia spoke for a long while, discussing the virtue of patience and how Kia would be wise

256

to go slower in her studies. She counseled that Kia should wait until she was older before she attempted certain dangerous things. Surprisingly, Kia agreed.

"You know best, Cacique," Kia said with a polite but insincere smile. "I will do as you say. Is there anything else?"

Molowia was not totally convinced by her sudden change of heart but wanted badly enough for it to be true that she accepted it. "No, nothing else, little one."

"Then I want to continue meditating now," Kia said. "Thank you for visiting me."

Uncertain, Molowia stood up. "Of course. I'll visit you again later."

"I will look forward to that," Kia said, not looking at her.

Molowia was tempted to look into the mind of Kia but chose not to do so. She knew Kia had become powerful enough to sense such an intrusion, and she didn't want to agitate an already dubious relationship.

She's just a child, she thought. *I must be tolerant. She'll grow and she'll learn.*

Kia, at that moment, was looking into Molowia's mind, and the old shaman did not detect the mental incursion.

Yes. I will grow and I will learn. I will learn many things. By Awona'Wiona, the miraculous things I will learn.

Hayoka walked across the Land of Everlasting Summer, unsure of what was happening back in Shipapa-Lina. As he crossed a devastated field, he wondered if the locusts had ravaged the Itiwana crops or destroyed the Tree of Life. He was afraid to go back to Shipapa-Lina. He might have to deal with the locusts, and even if they were gone, Calian and the Shakowin would accuse him of cowardice.

Where to go? he wondered. *What's next for me? Do I dare return to the Itiwana?*

Hayoka felt a sudden breeze blow past him. He looked to his feet and saw a handful of fallen leaves fluttering along the ground. The wafts of wind caused the leaves to swirl, forming a shape. The dead leaves formed an arrow, pointing the way to an unknown destination.

It took Hayoka a moment to realize what was happening. "Dagwona!"

Since she had warned him of danger, he chose to respond to her message. He marched in the direction the arrow indicated. Over the next hour, this strange scenario repeated itself four more times, guiding him to a particular destination. *Where is she leading me?*

After a long trek across plains that were mostly barren from the locust attack, he reached Manitou's Rise. Looking around, trying to deduce why he had been led there, he spotted the unmoving body in the grass.

Hayoka ran to examine the fallen woman and confirmed that it was indeed Dagwona. "Oh, by the gods!"

He cradled her bloodied body for a few moments, mourning her death, when her eyes shockingly opened. *She lives!*

"Life ... leaving," she weakly mumbled. "Dagwona ... dies!"

"No, I won't allow it," Hayoka said.

He lifted her in his arms. "I'll help you. Somehow, I'll help you. I won't let you die. There has to be a way to save you. By all the gods, I'll save you!"

CHAPTER TWENTY-SEVEN

Naya-Nazgani was still running rapidly through the northern fields and hills. He became angrier and more energized with every foot of his trek. Being a mastop-kachina, he didn't tire or slow. Nothing would deter him from reaching the fiends in time.

After a seemingly endless chase, he finally caught up with his prey. Three terrifying-looking skinwalkers were surrounding a bison with a harness and reins. The animal was apparently defending an unmoving man who lay prone in the grass.

"Leave him be!" a strong, authoritative voice yelled. "I'm the one you should be concerned with."

The three skinwalkers glared at the well-muscled man with the battle ax in his grip. The beasts focused their aggression on the newcomer, warning him away with fearsome growls. Their warnings had no effect on the monster hunter. The newcomer stared at the hybrid beasts with a look of anger that showed he had no fear of them. His stance and expression indicated his intention to fight.

Tawa, his eyes half-opened in a semi-conscious state, heard the voice of a mysterious savior. He had the belief that the Sky Elders had sent him an ally. *Thank you to whichever Elder sent me assistance.*

With a sneer, Naya-Nazgani held his ax in both hands, muscles flexing in preparation for combat. The skinwalkers all hesitated, sensing a formidable enemy. Naya-Nazgani walked slowly toward them and the skinwalkers all took a step back.

"You should have remained as mere human Antejini," Naya-Nazgani told them. "You chose wrongly when you chose to become monsters. That made you my enemy. No one else dies today. I won't allow it. No one human, at any rate."

Without further words, Naya-Nazgani, the monster hunter, leaped wingedly forward and swung his ax. Before the three skinwalkers could react, one of them had lost his head. A second tried foolishly to rush the formidable enemy head-on, only to have a hand cut off. A third attempted to sneak around behind Naya-Nazgani, flashing his claws with lethal intentions. However, the result was that the creature's arm was cut off, causing the Skinwalker to howl in pain and back away fearfully. It turned to flee but then felt the ax pierce its back. The monster's life ended in a spray of blood.

Naya-Nazgani closed in on the wounded final Skinwalker. The truth was that Naya-Nazgani loved killing monsters and felt the most alive when he was slaying strange beasts. It was what he did best. It was his life's purpose and his glory. No one did it better than Naya-Nazgani. He was the terrible swift ax of justice, and he always won.

As Naya-Nazgani ripped through the final Skinwalker like a shark tearing up some harmless fish, the blood was splattered all across the clearing. Looking down at his fallen foes, Naya-Nazgani raised his ax and cried a primal scream of victory and satisfaction. There were three fewer monsters in the world.

His heartbeat slowed and his breathing became softer. He looked down at the wounded man and approached non-threateningly. The big bison stepped closer, curious about whether this man was a danger to its master.

Naya-Nazgani petted the bison's nose and spoke gently. "Easy, big one. I'm a friend. I just want to help your master. I mean no harm. Be at ease."

His calm words and demeanor won over the bison, which allowed Naya-Nazgani to kneel beside Tawa. The monster hunter saw the open wound and the flowing blood. "This is bad."

"T... thank you," Tawa murmured.

"I feared I was going to be too late again," Naya-Nazgani said, studying the wound.

"Will I live?" Tawa asked. "The wound..."

"It isn't good," Naya-Nazgani said, putting pressure on the wound. "I must get you some help."

"Who ... are you?" Tawa managed to say.

"My name is Naya-Nazgani. I just came to kill monsters, but I am willing to spare the remainder of my day getting you to help."

"I am ... grateful," the dying man said. "My name is Tawa, chieftain of... of the Itiwana."

"Hello good chieftain," Naya-Nazgani said. "Save your breath. Let me help you."

Naya-Nazgani proffered no more words. He lifted Tawa up and placed him on the back of the bison. He made the Itiwana as comfortable as possible and then took the bison by the reins. He didn't take any notice of the golden arrow.

"Come along, big one," the monster slayer said. "Perhaps there is a close enough place to find help while your master still clings to life. He seems strong, and if fortune favors him, we may just save him."

EPILOGUE

In Shipapa-Lina, the Itiwana were hard at work repairing the damage that had occurred in recent days. The small, outer farms had been ravaged by the locusts and required assistance from their brothers and sisters of the Itiwana tribe. The burned wall of kindling had to be cleared away.

Since much of the forest around Shipapa-Lina had been devastated by the swarm, berries were going to be scarce until the forest replenished itself, but they did have a good surplus of nuts. Fortunately, the corn harvest was good, and they had buffalo meat. Now that the Whirlwind Witch was no longer a threat, the Itiwana fishermen could travel to the Pisas Vaya river to fish again.

Pahana had done a commendable job taking charge during this crisis. The Shakowin were happy with his performance as chieftain. He had vindicated himself. The Shakowin were especially happy since Hayoka had left the village. They hoped his absence would be permanent. Calian, in particular, was relieved about Hayoka's absence, but feared he had not seen the last of the son of Hobomok the Traitor.

Pinga continually kept a vigil, awaiting the return of her beloved Tawa. She told herself every day that he was alive and healthy and would be returning soon. Every night, as the moon rose, she retired disappointed. She often slept with a fire burning, so she could see if he entered their cliff chamber at night.

For so many years, This One has lived with the dread she may one day lose her love in battle, Pinga thought. *It has lurked like a phantom, a permanent blur in the corner of her eye. Now that it has been nudged to the center of my sight, it is like being ambushed by a grotesque.*

Others tell This One not to worry. That Tawa will return. But these are only words. Shades of truth that offer no consolation. I hope bold Tawa is as afraid for his life as This One is because sometimes fear can keep a man alive. Come back to us, my love. This One senses we have enemies approaching, the likes of which no man has ever seen. We need you. This One needs you.

The reddish sun took its nightly rest, leaving Shipapa-Lina in darkness. An ominous quiet settled over the Land of Everlasting Summer. The quiet before the thunderous storm.

Gunnar summoned the Dregnar, along with a man named Red Rolf, who was the nephew of the late Iron Forge—who had been killed by the Itiwana—and Grimhilt, the physically strongest of the young generation of Vykans. Gunnar led them to a secluded spot.

"I have gathered you worthies here because we four are charged with preserving the Vykan's honor as warriors without dishonoring the word of my father," Gunnar explained. "My father wants no war, and we will not debate his rightful commands at this moment. But might we four not go south to the land of the Itiwana and find the family of Tawa, the killer of Nanook and the Berserker? Might we not then win new glory for ourselves as warriors by bringing back the head of Tawa and his son? And since there will be no war, we will do so without defying my father's word. Are we agreed?"

The three Vykans readily concurred with young Gunnar. They would be an assassination party, not a war party, and they would show the Itiwana what happens when you dare harm one of the Vykan's dread lords. They'd show the scraelings the power of Vykan justice.

Far away, in the Spirit Fire Hill of the Shouting Mountains, an unsettling, ominous laugh echoed through the sweltering hot caves of the volcano. The gravelly, resonant laugh of Malsumis confirmed his delight in what his mystic visualizations were showing him. The path to his freedom was forming, just as he had hoped.

Soon! Very soon! A glorious war the likes of which no god or man has ever seen will tear this world asunder! The tree will fall, and Awona'Wilona will fall. Soon, another age of ice!

END OF BOOK TWO

COMING SOON/TEASER

I n **Book Three: The Valley of the Blue Mists**, Tawa, leader of the Itiwana, is lost and dying. He wants to see his loved ones before he dies. Far away, his son Pahana is settling into his leadership role, but is having trust issues due to the manipulative scheming of Hayoka. Pahana also finds himself faced with a dangerous new threat when the Itiwana tribe encounters the enigmatic community of shamans from the Valley of the Blue Mists. They take an interest in the rapidly growing mystic power of Tawa's daughter, Kia.

Pahana successfully protects his people from the latest threat sent by the Winter Elders, only to get word that his father is near death. Pahana must take it upon himself to continue his father's quest. But how can he succeed where even the great Tawa had failed?

AUTHOR BIO

R.J. Young has been everything from a dog groomer, to a custodian, to a hospital worker, but his one true love has always been writing. The son of an immigrant, he's had a life-long fascination with fantasy and sci-fi stories depicting exotic and astonishing locations. The first time he saw *The Wizard of Oz* at seven years old was a magical experience. A journalism major in college, he enjoys writing online reviews and articles. R.J. loves discussing fiction with anyone who will listen.

BOOK CLUB QUESTIONS

1. Is it right for parents to teach children to distrust and dislike certain people, due to the parents' personal views of those people?

2. Was Kia right to interfere in the war in order to protect her family, or did she have an obligation as the successor to Molowia to stay out of the war for the good of Kolhu?

3. Was Tawa right to leave Pahana to rule Shipapa-Lina in his absence, or had Pahana proven too irresponsible for such a responsibility?

4. Were the Shakowin too hard on Hayoka? Should they have given him the benefit of the doubt? Were they wrong to judge him because of what his father did? Is Calian justified in his suspicions?

5. Given the threat to her people, should Kia train with Shula-Witsa, despite his untrustworthy nature?

6. Many of the characters in this book feel pressure to live up to the reputation of their parents. Pahana, Calian, and Hayoka are all determined to prove their worth to their fathers, while Kia lives in the shadow of both her parents and Molowia. Is it fair to ask children to live up to such expectations, or is it necessary for them to step up, considering the danger the Itiwana face?